Journey to Nirvana

By
Douglas Fox

Journey to Nirvana

Cover photo: pawan-thapa-PIGJIBale70-unsplash.jpg

Spine photo: pixabay-swim-2754903_480.jpg (modified)

ISBN: 978-1-7923-9779-0

Library of Congress Control Number: 2022916202

BISAC: FIC028090, FIC028070, FIC028130

CONTENTS

Chapter One
A Sense of Purpose

John Forbes and Renee Jaspar sat side-by-side, snuggling right up against each other, holding hands, entranced as they gazed at the cool moonless night sky. The sky was subtly different, but they scarcely noticed. It was their last look, the last time it would look this way. Soon they would be sleeping, a long dreamless sleep as they accelerated far from their birth planet Gwydion Prime. Bright yellow and green dots faded quickly, planets of their system they would never see again. Ever-reddening stars mocked the denouement of the home they were so hastily and unexpectedly forced to leave, a shouting reminder of the friends and relatives they so sadly left behind. Every last one of them were likely dead by now. The two of them were left with only each other to fall back on, forming their own island of continuity, destined for a distant, unfamiliar, mostly unknown land. There would be no return flights. They were too overwhelmed, too dazed to look for the orange star they might one day call their own.

It was only now becoming real that the only place they had ever lived, all they had ever known, was not only gone, but gone forever. Before sleep walking to the shuttle that whisked them away, in the back of their minds, they could imagine a redemption, a last minute reprieve. But now, sadly and mournfully, almost mechanically, they recited their "Do you remember…", "Did you ever see…", "What about so and so…", "I remember when…" reminiscences one more time.

"Do you think we will survive the long hibernation? Will anything happen to us along the way? Do you think we will ever wake up again?" Renee asked.

"Let's be positive."

"But are you sure? What if one of us doesn't make it?"

"I'm sure. You know this ship and these systems better than I do. I just know the extreme care that went into designing and building it. Whatever happens, the two of us will face it together."

"Then hold me close. I want to remember this moment forever."

"As close as I can. We're explorers on an exciting adventure together. What do you think about 'the mission'?"

"Honestly, all I care about is the two of us here and now."

Yet, at least they were survivors, privileged to carry on and create the new future. They were the remnant, tasked with the grandest mission imaginable. They were the inheritors of the breathtaking, incomprehensibly vast, known universe, and possibly even the hidden magic of the rest of creation beyond anyone's ability to see. The enormity of it all, with its complex variations on basic themes, was breathtaking.

Commander Carson was surely right: what is the point of such a grand creation as this if there is no being, no intelligence, to see and understand it, to appreciate and experience it, and to merge into a cosmic oneness with it? What an incredible waste that would be!

Galacticus magnificus' quest to conquer the galaxy, to insure that in some corner of the cosmos an intelligence of the highest possible order remained aware, was the noblest possible enterprise. Success of their mission was mandatory, somehow, no matter how daunting the obstacles. The very salvation of the creation was at stake!

* * *

By the twenty-second century Earth's continents were divided into ten political blocs. Among them were the Sino-Asian bloc that included China, India, Southeast Asia, Australia, New Zealand, and Japan which was both the most populous and most powerful bloc, the Atlantic Alliance that included the former United States, Mexico, Central America, Canada, and Great Britain, and the South American bloc.

Galacticus magnificus had sent remote probes to nearby stars, including Earth's Sun, for several millennia before their endeavors were so unexpectedly cut short. To them, Earth was an inconvenient and temporary detour, a stepping stone where they would regroup, resupply, and resume their expedition. In order to continue their mission from Earth, they needed an in-orbit spacecraft assembly and launch facility, which in turn necessitated a cheap way to get payloads into orbit, namely space elevators like the ones they had built on their home planet.

As a precaution, two mother ships were launched from Gwydion Prime's smaller moon. One took a direct path to Earth, the other took a roundabout course that would expose it to different space hazards than the first. From there, the two ships would continue in different directions with the goal of populating two new home planets.

Upon their arrival, magnificus planned to establish two treaty-defined equatorial bases where they would build their elevators in different political jurisdictions. If it was necessary to send crew, rather than robots, to the planet's surface, Tasmania in Australia in the Sino-Asian bloc, and the area near Fargo, North Dakota in the Atlantic Alliance were two of the possibilities with habitable climates. Among their other benefits, these two locations had weather most resembling the temperate zones of their colder home planet. In this event, it might also be advantageous to reach an accord with Earth to build biologically isolated research and office facilities for magnificus at the two locations. At least, that was the plan.

* * *

Upon arrival in Earth orbit, the first order of business was to contact Earth's leaders to announce their presence and intentions. Detailed planning would then depend on what kind of a reception they got.

They determined that the most productive path would be to concentrate on the three most powerful blocs, the Atlantic Alliance led by Acting President Martin Wright, the Sino-Asian bloc led by President Liu Hyun, and the South American bloc led by Queen Antonia LaFuentes.

Carson tasked his reluctant second in command Van Newman and his assistant Murray Hooper to locate Earth network links they could tap into to initiate conversations with the key leaders. Then, to avoid the appearance of favoritism, he assigned Newman to contact Wright, Marie Lewis, chief diplomat and negotiator to contact Queen LaFuentes, and he himself contacted Liu, all simultaneously.

Carson began his conversation with Liu by saying "Hello President Liu, my name is Norman Carson, commander of a spaceship now in orbit…"

"Yeah, yeah, yeah," interrupted Liu, "I detected your ship on its way here a long time ago. Why did you think I wouldn't? It's too big to miss. Your crew Annie Koler already contacted me, so why are you bothering me again? Don't you coordinate your activities up there?" Liu admonished.

Carson was dumbfounded. Annie Koler? The fugitive computer hacker and weapons specialist? The felonious traitor? She should have been long since dead back on Gwydion Prime. Had she or some imposter stowed away somewhere onboard? Carson must get to the bottom of this, but first he had to think fast. He made up a story: "Koler was searching for network connections and was not authorized to speak with you or anyone else."

"Koler told me about your particle beam weapon. Before you threaten to destroy me with it, we already made a deal. She will provide me with the weapon codes and a link so I can use it, in exchange for meeting certain of her demands."

"This is news to me. What were her demands?" Carson had never intended for Earthlings to know about the four weapon carriers that accompanied them on their voyage. They were strictly a precaution for defensive measures, if necessary.

"I'm expecting to hear that from her once she decides what she wants."

"I can assure you that our weapon is secure and Annie is conning you," Carson bluffed.

"We'll see."

"I assure you, our weapon is strictly for our own protection and would never be used offensively."

"I already know better, so come clean. What are your real intentions? What are your orders?"

A computer-generated message popped up on Carson's screen: One of their two shuttles had defeated its security locks and left the mother ship, destination unknown. Carson quickly typed orders for the security computers while he continued his conversation with Liu.

"My orders are to establish two ground maintenance installations to refurbish our mission in exchange for transferring some of our technology to you that will find useful. What we can offer you is…"

"I'm not interested in your offer," Liu interrupted. "I'm only interested in Koler's deal."

"Koler is not authorized to speak or act for us."

"Then we have nothing more to talk about." Liu severed the connection.

Suddenly, Carson had urgent business finding out what was going on with Koler and the shuttle, and putting an end to it.

Meanwhile, Newman and Lewis completed their initial contacts, then the three of them met to compare notes and plan their next steps. Carson also briefed them with the news that Annie Koler had stowed away on a shuttle, which she had now stolen, and that she was trying to arrange her own deal with Liu.

Newman reported, "Computer checks establish that we have lost control of one of the weapons. Attempts to recall the escaped shuttle failed. Its control computer may have been hacked."

"What can we do about it?" Carson asked.

"The code for complex computer systems always contains an irreducible number of bugs and unanticipated interactions, even when they are programmed by other computers. That's why there are always back doors into every system. I have Hooper working on it. I'm sure we will find a way to regain control."

Several hours later, Liu re-established the call with Carson. Carson was in the middle of dealing with the Koler situation and took a minute to answer. But Liu always expected an immediate response, because that was only his just due.

"Why did you keep me waiting?" Liu demanded, his small dark eyes boring straight through his video image and into Carson like some kind of X-ray machine. "You know damn well my time is precious. I don't put up with this kind of treatment from you or anybody else."

"Please accept my apologies but we were in the middle of a planning session."

"That's no excuse. I won't tolerate your insubordination. Just what the hell did you think was so important that you had to put me off?"

"I will try to be more prompt in the future, Mr. President."

"Don't just try. I'm the leader of the most powerful bloc on earth and I can crush you and your Mickey Mouse space clutter anytime I damn well please. I am your highest and most immediate priority, understand? Can you get that straight before we proceed any further?"

"I will keep that in the front of my mind," Carson appeased.

"You had better do more than just 'keep it in mind'. The next time my secretary robot contacts you I expect you to jump. Now can we get on with the business at hand?"

"Certainly. What can I do for you?"

By now Carson's fur was starting to stand up.

Liu wore his customary well-tailored, perfectly fitting gray suit. He was a somewhat thin five-foot eight-inch brown-eyed black-haired firm-jawed presence. Liu spoke from the luxuriously appointed media office in his twenty-two thousand square foot Grand Palace, situated on a well-guarded and carefully manicured forty-acre tract. He spoke from behind his ornate one by two-and-a-half-meter teak media desk, a black, red, and white flag on its brass pole gracing the regal purple and white patterned sculpted walls behind him, everything trimmed with elaborate white enameled moldings.

A not so impressive, nearly naked in fact, brown and blonde furred, yellow-orange eyed, stocky five and a half foot tall Carson floated in his cramped and overflowing three-by-four meter plain beige office behind a metal desk, part of his administrative cubicle in the mother ship. The stark contrast between the two leaders suited Liu just fine, since it served to put the magnificus in their place, but irritatingly enough, they never managed to get the message.

"Did you make an offer to any of the other blocs?" Liu demanded.

"We thought it appropriate to talk to all of Earth's leaders at the same time. Our offer to them was the same as what I offered you. We explained that we wanted to establish a single agreement with all of Earth's jurisdictions."

"From now on, you are to deal only with me. You can promise me whatever you want, but I will dictate my terms when I find out more about you. I'm not going to commit to anything in advance. If

you want your maintenance and refueling base you have no choice but
to comply with my wishes."

* * *

The fat was about to slide into the fire.

Liu wanted proof that Koler controlled a weapon.

To accommodate him, Koler chose what she hoped was an
uninhabited small island in the southwest Pacific and destroyed it with
a full strength burst from the weapon she controlled. She at least knew
better than to ask Liu for the target, since it would on all likelihood be
owned or controlled by one of his rivals, sparking an international
crisis.

Liu could now press his demands.

"Carson, I've proven to you that Koler controls your weapon,
and I have a deal with her. You are now under my command now or
else I will turn the weapon on you, and you and your mother ship will
be history in the blink of an eye. Do you understand that?"

"If you had the weapon, you would already have destroyed us.
Annie isn't stupid. You will have to satisfy her and ensure her safety
first."

"Don't be so insolent. You have no say in the matter. That
should be simple enough that even a tiny little rat brain like yours can
figure it out. I order you to land at a location I will choose so I can
keep an eye on you. I may have a use for you and your ship."

"I'm sorry, but I have my responsibilities. I'm sure we can
work out a mutually satisfactory agreement."

"You're making me mad and when I'm angry somebody
always pays. What I do to you won't be my fault, capuche? I've had
more than enough of your gross disrespect. You have one day to
change your tune or I'll exterminate the lot of you like the rat vermin
you are. You're a sitting duck in orbit, with or without your weapon."

"I'm sure we can work something out."

"You try my patience. I'm giving you 24 hours to comply with
my orders. Goodbye."

What the Liu and the other Earth leaders didn't realize was that
there was not one but four laser-particle beam weapons in lunar orbit,

all with electromagnetic shields fully deployed, stacked in a row one behind another in an attempt to appear as a single entity. They also weren't aware that Annie had depleted a not insignificant amount of fuel from the weapon she had used.

They also didn't know about, or at least magnificus hoped they didn't know about, the fleet of fabrication-construction factory ships parked in one of Earth's Lagrange points, disguised as Trojan asteroids.

* * *

Carson's was responsible for informing his key staff of Liu's threats, once he found his comb to brush his short thick fur back down.

They all floated into the ship's small, stark beige-walled windowless meeting space.

Carson's appearance was typical of magnificus, males and females alike. Fur color might be brown, orange, yellow, occasionally ruddy, even a rare off-white. Males had but one or sometimes two colors, while females were multi-colored. Eye color was most often yellow or orange, complementary to the orange glow of the K2 star of their home planet. There were minor variations in height and weight.

"I got off the phone with Liu ten minutes ago," Carson explained in a rising voice, unusual for him. "He's claiming Koler is about to give him the weapon codes and demanding we become his subordinates and do his bidding. The way I read him, there's no possibility of an agreement or any compromise."

"You know these earthlings like to gamble, and if they are losing the bet they bluff. They will hide their true plans and motives until they can spring it on their opponents at the last second when it is too late for them to mount a defense." Dr. Bran Holland, a psychologist, said. "So can you judge if Liu is just gambling, bluffing, laying a trap or dead-serious if you will pardon the expression?"

"No, I can't. He was shouting and sounded like he meant it," Carson replied.

"Let's play their game for once," Newman suggested. "I'll program the remaining weapons to automatically retaliate if anything happens and we don't manually reset them every so often."

"Against what target?" Marie Lewis, chief diplomat and negotiator, asked.

"Does it matter?" Newman replied. "We're not going to tell Liu what the targets are; that's part of the deterrent."

"I don't want to resort to counter-threats. It's a vicious circle and I don't want to stoop to their level," Carson replied.

"Power and force might well be all he understands," Newman replied. "Humans are not even conscious of the impulses driving them from deep under the surface. Those impulses just throw them around like puppets. They don't play on a rational adult-being plane. I think we should consider the use of force. It's something all of them will understand."

"Our plan is to use diplomacy and involve all of the world's leaders." Lewis reminded them.

"That's Plan A, but when that fails? If there's no other way they have to comply. We total only 96. How can the few of us herd an entire planet-full of culturally splintered primitives with countless conflicting motives? It's a classic unpredictable complex system," Newman pointed out.

"So, let's be practical. I want to find out what their deepest, hidden motivations and conflicts are," interjected Dr. Holland. "Then we can pull their stings. We will be the master puppeteer."

"Maybe we're too late," Lewis interrupted. "Maybe there are powers behind the throne already pulling their stings. Then we have to pull the strings of the human puppeteers pulling the strings of the leaders. What a mess to deal with!"

"So we become manipulators and again stoop to their level?" Carson replied. "I can rule that out. Let me cut this short and remind everyone of the urgency of our mission," Carson continued. We and our other ship, which will arrive a year from now, are all that's left of magnificus. We are too few in number. If we fail, creation, the universe is doomed. It will all be meaningless. There is no other comparable intelligence that can grasp the greatness of it all. Earth has many options, but we don't. It means they hold all the cards. We need another plan, and it better be a good one."

"It might come down to the use of force, like it or not," Newman stated.

"I don't want to compromise our principles," Carson said.

"But," Forbes noted, "Sometimes nature reduces everything and everybody to the lowest common denominator. It comes down to fighting fire with fire. There are so many examples. In households where one of the members is an abusive narcissist or a criminal type everyone else walks on eggshells, tries to avoid the abuse, and shapes their lives around the bad behavior. In a political campaign where one candidate conducts a negative campaign, uses dirty tricks, distorts and smears the words and actions of the others, and receives more money for his campaign from questionable sources, the rest are compelled to follow suit or lose the battle. Spies are defended against by counterspies. Groups often come to be led by their most pathologically driven, power hungry member and every one else has to toe the line. Corruption works and is hard to root out. Spin and propaganda are effective. The examples are endless. It's amazing how one bad apple always controls the barrel. The situation could easily degenerate due to only one or two bad actors."

"Let's hope it doesn't come to that," Carson insisted.

"What are your orders, then?" Lewis asked.

"We are going to make a list of possible plans and start to flesh them out and look at contingencies for each," Carson directed. "Then we'll go from there."

"I just want to remind everybody about the fallacies of dealing with alien cultures. They will naturally assume our civilization is like theirs and we have the same motivations and values. Then they will grossly miscalculate and misinterpret, and things will go off the rails," Lewis persisted. "Of course, we ourselves know every planet is different and has a unique history, so we can guard against the same mistake."

"Yes, yes, of course we all know this." Newman was impatient.

"Does that mean Liu will set us up as a scapegoat to boost his own ambitions?" Lewis persisted. "I would like to consider a public relations campaign. Plant a story about us they want to hear, promote the memes that gain their support, sell our story. Spin is what counts in earth society. They will listen to whatever flatters their emotions and promotes their ambitions. Let's espouse something they want and become a role model they aspire to."

"That's not a plan in itself, but maybe it's a strategy that will help our cause," Carson judged. "Give me a detailed action list in two days."

Forbes added, "We can't help disturbing their status quo, so either we're a means to their own ends or they get rid of us. There's a lot we could do for them with our advanced technology but some of them won't want we can offer and will try to neutralize us somehow. It's a multi-dimensional chess match."

Carson concluded, "A complex multi-faceted game, indeed. Jaspar, you are our senior engineer. What do you know about game theory and game strategy?"

"Not in the curriculum," Jaspar replied. "Does anyone have the manual?"

"I'm sure you can find one," Carson replied. "Looks like you have an all-night cram session coming up."

"Marie, what are the reactions of the other leaders to Koler's attack on the island?" Carson asked Lewis.

"I'm afraid it put Earth on notice we can attack them and cause severe damage, so now there isn't much trust. They suspect we're a wolf in sheep's clothing. We have to regain control of the weapon, convince them we have it, and find a way to establish trust. As long as Koler controls the weapon, she has both a carrot and a very big stick."

"The weapons have their safeguards and my staff is looking at a backdoor to regain control," Newman stated.

* * *

Everyone drifted out except Carson, Newman, and Forbes.

"Something has been bothering me," Carson observed. "We've never talked to anyone except Liu, Taylor, Mason, LaFuentes, Mitchell, and the other political leaders. They don't allow us any other contacts. We see activity from orbit, but has anyone seen a single human worker? Robots do everything. They're the builders, the miners, and the workers. I'm getting the strong impression something is hidden."

Maybe we only see a façade," Newman replied. "Or to the contrary, maybe that's all there is. We still have two of our three old exploratory interplanetary probes that remain here, almost fully functional in high orbit, watching and listening to their broadcast communications, and gathering intelligence, using their onboard AI computers to analyze the data."

"Why don't you follow that up and see where it leads?" Actually, that wasn't a question. It was one of Carson's orders.

"Let *me* suggest our next steps," Newman interrupted. "First, we try to use the surveillance and AI computers to determine the supposed and actual forms of government and lines of command. We figure out who really runs what around this place and what their hidden agendas are. On a broader level, the surveillance computers are trying to ferret out prevalent unspoken and probably unexamined beliefs by culture and subculture, along with Earth's current memes that we have to take into consideration. Since we have so little collective manpower, I have to maximize the use of our computers. I want our AI to help us to focus our approach where it gives the most leverage. As soon as our plans are completed, we can refine our strategy for getting our space elevator complexes built, since that's our top priority."

"Agree."

Forbes wanted to add a detail to the analysis. "I've been comparing scans of the planet our probes made a hundred and fifty Earth years ago to the current scans, and there in fact *are* some interesting differences. There is an enormous hotspot on an island in the middle of the Pacific Ocean. It radiates a great deal of heat, there are permanent towering water vapor clouds above it, and we've also detected a very small amount of radioactivity, mostly neutrons, protons, and high energy gamma rays. Much smaller, similar hotspots are present on islands just off the West coast of North America, the North Coast of South America, and Southeast Asia. Some lesser hot spots are also scattered on half a dozen islands elsewhere around the world. None of these features existed in the earlier scans. I think volcanic activity is picking up on the planet."

"What about eruptions, lava flows, earthquakes, tsunamis, and other geologic activity?" Newman asked.

"On average, about the same as before."

"Do you think there is any immediate danger we have to watch out for?" Carson inquired.

"No, I think it's just something to monitor for now."

* * *

Carson reassembled his key staff two days later in the morning. "Do you have the summary intelligence report you promised?" he asked Newman.

Suddenly there was a loud bang and a flash of light, then five seconds later another bang. The entire station shook.

"What the?" Forbes exclaimed.

"Hit the deck! Either we're under attack or our cold fusion reactor just malfunctioned," Newman coolly stated. "Judging by the fact that the lights are still on I would opt for the former."

"It's just like what happened during our approach to orbit," Carlson exclaimed as he lurched up to the ceiling. "Are our defenses still working?" Furry magnificus bodies floated and ricocheted everywhere.

"Anti-missile and anti-asteroid lasers and particle beams operational; deflection shields deployed, or what's left of them," a disembodied voice announced over the intercom.

"What's our safest action now?" Lewis asked in an unsteady voice as her plump wide-eyed brown and white furry body disappeared under the large table in the middle of the room.

"Everybody crowd in the middle and stay put," Carson said. "Just wait a few minutes. We don't know what kind of radiation might be penetrating and the levels."

There was a loud explosion outside. Thick black smoke became visible from the east porthole.

"Either it's over or we're all dead. I'll query the surveillance fleet and try to find out where this came from," Newman said as he fingered his hand-held computer.

"Incoming detonated," the disembodied voice droned on.

An acrid smell started to infiltrate the ship. "Laser overload," the annoying voice said flatly.

"See if it was an attack and where it came from. If it was an attack, we have no choice except to push back," Carson stated. "If we don't retaliate, they will feel free to escalate their attack."

After a pause Newman stated, "Surveillance detected and neutralized two incoming missiles launched from a point in the Korean peninsula. Suggest we have our computers direct one of the particle beam weapons to the launch site and take it out."

"Bridge, return fire, Newman's coordinates. Minimum heat. Just a warning, no escalation," Carson ordered.

"I can guess who's responsible for this," Carson added. "It's time for a chat." Just then his phone started to flash. He answered it at once.

"President Liu, please stand by." Carson recognized the voice of Liu's right hand man Theodore Mitchell.

"Just what was the point of that?" Carson immediately asked Liu.

"The point is, your time is up. That was your only warning. Next time you won't be in a position to answer my call. You're a rat on a sinking ship unless you order Koler to hand over your weapon."

"All you did was prove why we have to remain in control of it. Newman reprogrammed it to wipe *you* out if we don't manually reset it periodically."

"If you think you can brush me off that simply you're badly mistaken. I can easily crush your simple-minded ploy."

"That's up to you. We're still ready to conclude an agreement."

"You say you want an agreement?" Liu pretended. "You want to build a space elevator and I have the only politically stable location on the equator in Rengat, Sumatra, Indonesia. Give me your weapon and I will grant you the site and the infrastructure you need. Otherwise, your hours are numbered. Start counting on your fingers. You won't get to twelve."

"Please consider that a space elevator will be a lucrative money-maker for both of us. It can put payloads into orbit for a fraction of a percent of the cost of using rockets. Consider the expertise and engineering we can provide you with. As far as the site goes, though, Indonesia is a geothermal hotspot and you don't have a perfect location."

"You are so infuriating I'm fed up with you. You have my terms. I don't give damn about your space elevator and neither does anyone else on this planet. The only thing that gets launched these days are government payloads, and I'm the government. Nobody gives a rat's ass about what you need except you, so you better play ball."

Carson wondered what was so valuable about rodent buttocks. After all, he most earth land creatures had them. "I'm afraid that might be interpreted by other leaders as an act of war."

"That's enough of your squirrelly logic. Give me what I want or you won't remain here for long, it's as simple as that."

* * *

"What is this pre-occupation the humans have with rats and mice and squirrels? Now Liu is calling us 'squirrelly'," Forbes said.

"Maybe they're descended from squirrels and its part of their deep unconscious Holland was talking about," Newman said.

"You're saying that in their subconscious they think of us as extraterrestrial rodents?" Lewis asked.

"Well, I *did* see Forbes out in the woods collecting nuts back on our home planet, and he was one of the furriest creatures there," Holland said. "I also happen to know he rented a pair of humongous front teeth."

"Very funny," Forbes responded. "It so happens I was just collecting some nuts and all of them ended up here on this ship."

Chapter Two
A Day in the Life

A souped up mini-Cooper was well in the lead, could you believe it? Joseph Witherspoon had the fastest car, a Lotus; he traded up for it with the rewards from previous races he had won. Was he having a bad day, taunted by the mini? Hardly; he felt like he was on top of his game, but the mini-Cooper was fast through the short streets and sharp turns of the towns, and its small size allowed it to cut through alleys none of the other cars could fit through, shaving miles off its course. He didn't like being in second place, and almost as bad as that he had a Nissan, a Ford, and a Chevy right on his bumper. That damned Ford! The two of them finished in a dead heat in the last race, denying Joseph the championship he worked so hard for this past year. Joseph wanted revenge!

Joseph Witherspoon hit the gas as he was finishing the turn out of the main street onto the highway, tires screeching, engine whining and revving at max RPMs, the head of a train with the yellow Nissan following right on his tail, drafting him, followed by the red Chevy drafting the Nissan, followed by the blue and white Ford drafting the Chevy, all opening up to full throttle. He speed shifted to high gear, chasing the mini-Cooper a quarter mile ahead. He didn't know the driver of the ridiculous looking mini, the little car with a small V8 crammed into the modified and enlarged engine compartment, bursting to explode out the front of the midget car.

Suddenly metal parts were flying everywhere; the mini-Cooper blew up, it's overstrained mini-engine spewing rods and fuel pumps and shrapnel all over the road. "Grip the wheel tight," Joseph told himself, better not run over anything, don't blow a tire and lose the race! Don't pass over a sharp piece of metal he reminded himself, or the draft from his fast-moving car might kick it up to puncture his oil pan.

Joseph swerved back and forth, momentarily taking his foot off the gas then reaccelerating, dodging the debris, the Nissan tight on his rear the entire time. "He's on your bumper, block his visibility, head for some shrapnel then swerve out of the way at the last minute leaving him to run over it," he said to himself. "BANG!" Mission accomplished! Two of the Nissan's tires burst as it skidded off the road and flipped over into a ditch. Joseph poked his one-button auto-text. "2 bad teach u a lesson Jack keep off my butt!!!" it said to the Nissan.

Joseph was still in the lead. Now it was the Ford behind him followed by the Chevy. He hit his one button auto-text again sending "Up yours Tony!!!" to the Ford. "Bend over Joseph!!!" was the reply.

"Dammit! Crap!" he suddenly swore as a pedestrian from nowhere stepped out onto the road right dead ahead of him. Joseph jerked the wheel and tapped the breaks, breaking traction with his rear wheels, deftly spinning the car around in a 360, barely avoiding the pedestrian but coming to a complete stop facing backwards in the process. The Ford and the Chevy flashed right by. "Eat my dust!!!" flashed across his console from the Chevy. Hitting a pedestrian would not only disqualify him from the race, but bust him all the way back to rookie status and put him in an inferior car. He slammed the shift into first gear while turning the wheel, straightening it as he accelerated and aimed his car towards the quickly fading Ford and Chevy, rifling through the gears, pedal to the floor. Nobody could handle a Lotus the way he could.

All he could do was accelerate as fast as the car would allow, the master of the gears and the gas that he was, trying to close and catch them before the labyrinth of the next town. Then up ahead, two blocks before the end of the highway straightaway he saw a traffic light, turning yellow. Would it catch them? Yes! They had to stop! Violating a red light, or for that matter going the wrong way on a one way street, failing to stop at a stop sign, and any other infraction except speeding incurred a costly time penalty. "Time it! Time it! Watch the color of the light on the side street. Ease up a bit, make it just right…" he told himself as he slowed, gauging his speed, reduced now to a leisurely seventy-five. The side street light turned yellow. "Three point eight seconds, that's the average yellow time, go for the three point eight," he said to himself. If he entered the intersection while it was still yellow, he would suffer a ten-minute time penalty and lose the race. Hit it just right and he could gain a three-block lead. One lane street ahead. "Yes! Perfect! You are so good!" he exclaimed to himself. The light turned green exactly as he stormed through the intersection at seventy, the other two cars at a dead stop. "Stick it Charlie!!!" was his message to the Chevy.

The Chevy was falling behind. Now the race was again between him and the Ford, just like last time. "Give it up now Tony ur fried!!!" he sent to the Ford. "Say ur prayers Joseph!!!" was the reply.

He memorized the street maps of the towns they raced through. They all did. The route through each town was up to the drivers. Unexpected traffic jams, accidents, police chases, work zones, broken down cars and trucks, long backups from cars lined up to get to the big sale at the shopping mall, some of those always cropped up suddenly; you had to react immediately, deciding on the best alternate route without hesitation or you had no chance of winning. Total concentration.

Joseph suddenly slammed on his brakes and swung the tail of his car ninety degrees counter-clockwise in a hard left turn onto a city street. He could see columns of tail lights three blocks ahead but he was ready. Right in two blocks to an alternate route and gave out a warning blast on his horn. Full speed through residential streets was risky and many a driver wiped out on cars pulling out of parking places, or crashed into unannounced construction work, or they rammed emergency vehicles running lights and the like. He lost track of the Ford and Chevy. Did they have better routes? Did they avoid the obstacles?

Finally, Joseph emerged from the town and onto the final two miles of interstate, dodging a funeral procession and outrunning a cop who took chase behind. At least this time the cop wouldn't be catching him to write a ticket and costing him time, or calling for backup to trap him in the next town like what happened to him earlier in his racing career.

But where was the Ford? Joseph pushed the button, taunting it with the phony message "It's all over for you sucker, I crossed the line," or did the Ford or Chevy already finish ahead of him? Then his race was over but the adrenaline hadn't diminished even slightly. He took his car to impound for a final technical inspection, but he knew it was legal and he hadn't cheated. Ninety-five per cent of the time the computer would catch cheating and it wasn't worth the risk unless you were desperate.

After ten minutes that seemed like forever, the announcer, who looked curiously like President Liu, blared out "The winner of the Grand National Championship Race is Lotus car number ninety-seven. Second place is Ford car number twenty-two. Third place is car number fifty-six. Nine finishers in the field of twenty-nine." He did it! National Champion! The four-hour marathon race was over already; it was so intense, so exhausting, but so satisfying, and yet it seemed too brief. He had won at the highest level. "Congrats" was the message from Tony; "Nice job, cracked up in town" was the message from Charlie.

Now he could retire at the pinnacle and garner the prizes coming his way. It was sad to hang up his helmet and racing suit and to say goodbye to most of the racing buddies he had gotten to know on a daily basis, but at least there would be occasional memorial races with other former champions, the greats of the racing circuit. Tony was probably destined to join a few of them in the racing hall of fame.

It was one of the best days Joseph had in a long while. Now it was time for dinner. In elation over his final victory Joseph added strawberry shortcake to his dinner order. "Hello Mickey," he said as his cat jumped on his lap to congratulate him, or was it because it was meal time?

Every apartment had a mini-kitchen with an automated food preparation system. Feedstock was delivered serially to the machines through four government-controlled pipelines with the approved ingredients in the correct proportions. The meal he ordered was piped in, 3D printed, and delivered to heating and refrigerator-freezer units for final processing, entirely without human intervention. The texture, flavor and appearance of the food, which had been perfected in government laboratories, was always consistent and exactly what Joseph wanted. He was a steak-and-potatoes kind of guy, and that is what he had ordered up that morning in anticipation of doing well in his race. After eight minutes of splooshes, whirs, grinds, and bangs it was ready, spat out onto one of the plates he preloaded into the machine.

He logged onto his computer as he was finishing the last of his shortcake. A Chattertwit message was waiting for him from Tony. "Congrats u bastard. I'm happy ur out of the racing scene so I don't have to worry bout u next time." He immediately typed back "Thank u I know u will b next natl champ."

"Saw what u did 2 the Nissan. Dirty tricks again"

"Alls fair"

"U eliminate 1/2 your competition that way every time"

"Never 2 u. Within the rules"

"The other drivers copy ur tricks"

"Who?"

"All. Role model"

"Thx"

"Not for me"

"U'll learn. Feel good bout it"

"Maybe. Good luck. Bye"

Joseph hadn't had a chance to update his Mugbook page yet. There was no time to lose. He wanted everyone to know about his success right away and added photos from his race along with the comment, "New National Champion." But before adding his pictures he had to Imageshop and Voiceshop them to display the social network appearance he wanted. His racing persona, Joe Flash, the image the rest of the world knew him as, was a self-assured, trim, blonde haired blue-eyed square-jawed six-foot hunk who would stride confidently to the podium to accept his virtual trophy. Not to worry, the neural networks in his image software had long since learned how he wanted to appear and sound. All Joseph had to do was apply some minor tweaks.

He also sent a Chattertwit message to his son, now eleven and a half years old. He had only seen Imageshopped photos of him since the last time they were together when he was three, but they corresponded three or four times a week.

"Hi Jonas won championship race. U can b proud of ur father. How was ur test?"

"Dunno felt OK"

"Did u show an aptitude?"

"Tried to show em I can b game tester"

"Good luck, hope they bite, know ur good at it"

"What if not?"

"Don't worry, very happy about the job they gave me, didn't think I would"

Age eleven and a half was a crucial time; that was when the government gave academic and social intelligence and aptitude tests to all children. The results determined the kind of work they were assigned to do and the education and training they would receive from then on, although there was an appeal process to retake a test. There was also a pretest at age four and a half once children were fully weaned from their parents' custody, to detect any special aptitudes useful to the government that required training to start young.

At eleven, Jonas was still not considered an adult. He had not yet fully developed the catalog of personas and avatars he would need to function in cyber-society, so an exchange of thoughts and feelings with his father was still occasionally possible.

Joseph had one other child, a daughter named Megan, now twenty. He texted her every week or so.

A message from Joseph's robot handler read "Good work. An email will explain your bonuses."

Now it was time to move on. He was still too excited to sleep so he took a pill and dozed off soon thereafter.

* * *

A gentle female voice prompted him "Joseph, rise and shine, time to get up, time to begin your day..." That was the que for a certain gray and white four-legged furry creature to jump on the bed and snuggle up to his face. "Mornin', Mickey," Joseph said to his virtual cat as he started scratching its ears. This was no dumb cat. It knew the voice in the alarm meant breakfast would soon be served.

It didn't take much to get Joseph up, in fact he could hardly wait for morning. His mildly overweight five-foot nine-inch brown eyed, brown-haired frame bounced out of bed. Most people were outwardly satisfied with their lives. As the announcers often reminded them, modern life was so much easier and more fulfilling than that of their ancestors. They were all so lucky.

Of course, the first order of business was to deliver the newly dispensed virtual cat food to the bowl on the floor.

Joseph himself decided to accept the breakfast he had selected the previous evening rather than wait around for a new feed. He enjoyed scrambled egg substitutes with pseudo-sausage, hash browns, and coffee with non-dairy creamer and sugar, though of course everything not only tasted like the real thing, but every flavor was chemically enhanced.

He dressed and got ready for today's three-hour work shift, then petted his cat for a minute before exclaiming "See you later, Mickey" and leaving, taking the elevator to his waiting robo-truck at ground level.

Today's assignment was to replace cracked insulators atop a high voltage transmission tower. It was a dangerous job, but then he looked forward to the extra tokens he earned from such hazardous work. The job could be done by robots, but why would anyone risk a crippling high-voltage shock to an expensive robot? These kinds of jobs had to be carried out by humans.

The sparsely travelled underground streets had their share of ruts and weren't in the best of shape. Most of the traffic consisted of robo-trucks in all different sizes. They easily absorbed the bumps and jolts.

The truck pulled off the road and proceeded slowly along the bumpy right-of-way of the high voltage lines. On arriving at the problem tower Joseph climbed into the truck's bucket and was lifted to the height of the lower pair of insulators, checking the electro-magnetic readings as he rose up to make sure no power was being transmitted through the wires. At the same time another worker was lifted up to the lower pair of insulators on the other side. Both of them went through the process of supporting and then disconnecting the wires, replacing the insulators, and then replacing the wires, all with the help of cranes extending from other trucks next to them. Then they repeated the process for the upper pairs of insulators. Upon returning to the ground the robots automatically and remotely restored power and tested the circuits. These particular transmission lines were old and not superconducting. Of course, Joseph didn't talk to the coworker on the other side of the tower, since neither of them had a cellphone or notebook computer with them on the job to text with.

Sorry to say, one of Joseph's Mugbook buddies was killed in a high voltage accident less than a month before. It was sad, although hundreds turned out for the cyber-funeral.

* * *

Inch-by-inch, robots took over most jobs. Robots had the further advantage that once one of them was trained or programmed to do a task, that training could be immediately downloaded to the others, and experience and knowledge gained by one robot could thus be quickly and automatically transferred to the rest. People performed only some high level and some low-level work.

Simple and semi-skilled manual jobs where it was cheaper to use a human than bear the cost of investment in a sophisticated robot were still handled by people. Examples of these low level, low status jobs were plumber robot and electrician robot helpers, robot handyman assistant, robot chef assistants (for example, food tasters), robot doctor assistants, jobs requiring special senses such as sewage plant operators, animal handlers such as for dogs trained to look for and follow scents, and some kinds of manual labor.

Dangerous jobs that could result in damage or crippling of a robot were also carried out by humans, all of them low level jobs such as construction beam walkers and high voltage workers. These jobs at least rewarded the workers with substantial hazardous duty tokens.

A few one-of-a-kind jobs were not worth the development and training cost of a robot and still needed people.

Human robot overseers were in demand, especially for monitoring decision-making artificial intelligence robots and computers. These jobs were more skilled and demanded special training and education.

What robots initially did poorly were jobs that took into account purely human factors. That was in spite of their incorporation of mathematical models of human emotion and behavior, which were seldom closely congruous with the real thing. Computers could not easily read human intentions; predict culturally influenced human values; discern deep unconscious drives, instincts, motives, desires, and conflicts; tell when a person might come to a breaking point, an insight, or a dysfunctional state such as depression or despair; detect all forms of deception although some facial expressions and physiological signs could be read and can serve as a hint; distinguish humor, mental play, most forms of devious behavior, disguised intent, or misdirection whether this arises from real intent or subconsciously driven compulsions, although computers could detect logical inconsistencies that may or may not be a clue to such deception; nor could computers evaluate the results of innovative and creative processes as to how directly useful they are to people.

Child monitoring and care of elementary aged children had turned out to require occasional human assistance and so was not purely a robot job and was one of the few occupations that entailed limited direct human contact.

Music and literature were other examples. Inspired composers can create music that touches the heart or that paints a picture or sets a dramatic scene, all in the composer's distinctive and expressive style. Computers couldn't do that in any satisfying way. Programs were robotically written that break down the works of a composer statistically and apply the rules of music theory to create music that unmistakably imitates the composer's sound. But there was no overall architecture to the music, no logical build to a climax and drive to a conclusion, no grand structure, no overwhelming feeling the music focuses on. Nor can computers impart the emotional expression and nuances to music the way a gifted performer can. In other words, robotic music cannot strike a deep emotional chord or invoke a profound sense of meaning and self. It lacks a soul.

Similarly for literature. Robo literature and automated plot generators can mimic a writer but miss the essence of his style and expression. Again, there is no human feeling.

However, robotic music and literature does have very practical uses: using a writer's works, or the works of a composer as performed by professional musicians, computers can economically use statistical and other techniques to generate adequate background music, advertising copy, or propaganda in endless variations. A human can sort through the results to pick out the most psychologically effective versions.

Most human feeling centered jobs had occupied a higher level in society's informal caste system. They included, for example, athletes (although nearly all athletic contests were now virtual and were staged as participatory computer games); bedside specialty nurses; investigative or police interrogators; non-robotic and non-automated TV hosts; fashion designers and hairdressers; social event planners; psychologists and other jobs requiring social intelligence or human intuition; jobs based on deception, guile, or bluff such as propagandists, spin doctors, advertising executives, and political strategists; artists and art critics; artistic photographers; landscape designers; architects designing the overall esthetics of a structure; entertainers and caregivers to the elite; advice columnists, astrologers, and palmists; law enforcement officers who must judge people's reactions and intent; and spiritual leaders. Attempts by the government to eliminate prostitutes or replace them with robots and simulations had so far been notably less than successful.

But all of this was before the bootstrapping revolution. As robots reprogrammed themselves and exchanged improved algorithms with each other, they taught themselves to mimic particular individuals much more accurately. They could now take photographs including facial expressions and body language, recorded conversations, personal histories and diaries, memoirs, news stories, DNA combined with epigenetics, and a host of other sources and meld them into images that looked and acted like the actual person, such that hardly anybody could tell it was a simulation. But while machines could closely mimic a human's persona, modeling and simulating the true self behind the persona was still a work in progress.

The most elite jobs were those of computer assisted game designers, game testers, and neurochemical engineers.

Finally, at the top of the job heap there were the entrepreneurs, human and robotic, and those who oversaw the conceptualization, design, manufacture, training, and deployment of the robots, games, and social media tools that comprised the key part of society and the economy.

Naturally, Joseph and his fellow plebs never thought much about all this. They were completely consumed by their day-to-day social, gaming, and job activities.

Joseph returned home to the best part of the day, the entire point of everyone's existence. His underground one bedroom, one bathroom apartment was comfortable enough and unusually spacious, if plain, with its beige walls, plush faux leather couch and chairs, chrome and glass tables, gold-colored draperies, huge L-shaped computer desk with its comfortable ergonomic swivel chair, and a giant holographic screen. There was a large faux window in the living room and a small one in the bedroom that seemed to look out at other buildings and a sunny side street. There was also a cozy but functional kitchen with a dining nook, and there was ample closet space. His winnings provided more than enough tokens to pay the rent.

Now it was time to grab a quick bite, lay out some energy snacks and drinks next to the console, go to the bathroom, and pet Mickey and make sure he had water and some dry food in his bowl. Joseph wouldn't be getting up from his swivel chair for the next four hours.

Since he had risen to the top of the racing game and claimed the crown, he had to move on and find a new game. What kind of adventure should he start next?

Joseph chose a multi-player role-play game, the kind he preferred, "Dogs of the Holy Grail". He was entering an entirely new virtual life that would completely swallow him as he learned and honed his new skills, leveling up, climbing his way to the top step-by-step.

Here he was, at the bottom of the heap, a skill level zero newbie, forced to start out as a lowly squire to the ill-equipped knight Sir Sidney in the currently small and threatened Kingdom of Old Dogbite. In fact, it would be up to him to succeed in assignments that would provide Sir Sidney with better armor and a decent sword. His six-foot blonde, blue-eyed avatar was clothed only in rags with a short rusty knife tucked into the rope around his waist, but he did not have to labor alone; there were other squires and knights, all of them more experienced than he. He could form temporary alliances with them, but he had better mind the fleeting clues and watch out for the double-crossers, lest they take what meager, inadequate weapons, clothes, and shelter he began with entirely away. They would climb over him on their way up if they had to, and he would do the same to them.

Once the game started, he was locked in for the full four hours. Any pause might mean losing points or failing to get his best score. Mickey was curled up on the couch. He was ready.

And it began! He was with his knight and master Sir Sidney in his Lord's rickety castle, surrounded by a hostile, superior army of mutant Invisigoths. Not surprisingly, the Lord of the castle was beholden to a King who looked exactly like President Liu's resplendent avatar, unusually tall and muscular, with its square jaw and caped purple heroic pose. (Villains were usually the avatars of political foes.)

What was his assignment? What was it he had to do to avoid almost certain doom? Nobody could tell him! He had to figure it out for himself, and fast, before the menacing army encroached any further. The strategy was to first search around for something, anything out of place, then scour the castle for players who were in the wrong place or shouldn't be there at all. He would also search for a soothsayer, fortune tellers, seemingly old senile residents who had secret knowledge and weren't what they appeared to be. It would all come as riddles, puzzles to be solved, something that was out of place or not quite right that he had better notice and investigate.

Too soon the gaming period was over. Now it was time to eat and log onto Mugbook. He connected with the Dogs of the Holy Grail player community and started a chat with Rover267.

"Me Squire4137 newbie 'Holy Race' champ, u?"

"Aint no race, wat level u on?"

"Still 0"

"Only 0? Made 1 my first day"

"Don't believe u"

"Ur avatar is 2 shabby"

"Have tokens, wat 2 buy?"

"How many u earned?"

"6"

"Wat can u get?"

"Steel sword for knight, new dagger or armor for avatar, or get more tokens and magic sword, wat u think?"

"Ur problem"

"U know, tell me"

"Go figure it out"

"Some frend"

"We all have 2. U won't catch me"

"Will 2"

Joseph was ready to teach this obnoxious, smug jerk a lesson starting tomorrow. Just then he got a Chatterbuzz from his friend ElectroWiz481.

"Hear about Wayne43?"

"Yes wat happen?"

"Current on premature. U go 2 cyberfuneral?"

"Yes"

"Worried? Ever happen 2 u?"

"No sweat. Know my job. Big bonuses. U?"

"I worry"

Someone interrupted, "Hey Joseph"

"Wat u want Tony?"

"U made this wk gamer honor roll, c it?"

"No but well deserved"

"Shut up"

He saw his avatar, not just on the weekly honor roll but in the Holy Race winner's circle. For some reason, as he looked at it, it didn't really seem like himself. Once again, things didn't feel right. It was all a hollow pose. Only Mickey the mouser sensed who he really was; he didn't even know and felt like a stranger to himself. "Snap out of it!" he told himself. "What kind of silly thinking is this anyway? Tomorrow I go for level 1."

Joseph's daughter, who was recently engaged, was Chattertwitting him.

"How's ur fiancé? He is neurochemical engineer right?"

"Yes"

"U make a great power couple. Im so proud ur a computer applications director like ur mom"

"Thank u. Daddy, I want a real wedding, not a virtual wedding, but Im scared. He's only seen my Mugbook Imageshop photos. He'll find out what I really look like and sound like. He might c my real personality. My Mugbook picture is tall slender brown hair blue eyes long blowing hair and maybe skimpy wardrobe like my avatar."

"I know sweetheart, it's risky. It usually means losing the relationship. That's why hardly anybody has 1. Dont think u should do it"

"U think I should just have a virtual wedding?"

"Pls. Real 2 risky but u have 2 decide wat u want. Is it worth it 2 u 2 risk losing him? Remember ur only 20. U have plenty of time ahead of u to find another"

"O daddy, Im not sure. Don't want to upset u or mom"

"Hundreds can come 2 ur cyber wedding but only 1 or 2 or maybe nobody 2 real. Is that wat u want?"

"Im confused"

"How strong is ur relationship?"

"I luv his persona so very much and he luvs mine 2"

"If u intend 2 have conjugal visit with ur husband when u get ur baby license instead of artificial, u risk a divorce then 2"

"I don't know if I would, I mean if it's virtual wedding I'll probably have artificial insemination and virtual sex every1 else I know"

"Wat does ur fiancé say?"

"He wants real wedding. Dont want 2 disappoint him"

"Does he insist on it?"

"Yes but maybe he will change his mind"

"Wat about ur mother?"

"She thinks Im crazy, doesn't understand y anyone in right mind would go real. Thinks real is 4 losers"

"Yes real always 4 losers. Y don't u let it simmer a couple weeks and c if u feel any different?"

"Maybe I should"

* * *

Joseph's schedule was fixed by convention and controlled by the authorities. The average citizen worked two to five hours a day, played computer games for four hours, ate their meals, and then went online with their favorite social media the rest of the time.

The games were really the thing; everyone was addicted and that's how they all wanted it.

If you did well and focused and immersed yourself you would be rewarded with Humbelixent. Nobody knew what the drug was, but it made people happy, improved their concentration and commitment to the games, and made them crave more.

The buzz that came from even small victories was known as "fiero," an uncontrollable addiction to winning, the overpowering feeling one gets after triumphing over adversity. It came in continuing doses large and small, not like the fleeting, rare moments of triumph life in the real world brings. With each player working at the limit of their ability, the regular small triumphs and the even more frequent near-misses were exhilarating and addictive.

With all sanctioned games, results, feedback, and gratification were immediate. This was called "flow," a continuous feeling of creative accomplishment and heightened functioning, and it was intense, totally absorbing. There was never a need to sacrifice immediate gratification for the sake of long-term success. Patience was no longer a virtue.

Neither were there any exhausting, pressure filled two-to-five-year projects, no days or weeks of setbacks, no boring meetings, no screaming bosses, no delayed rewards, no dead ends, none of that. It was all fast action and instant gratification. Computers adjusted the difficulty of games so they were just at the edge of the players' current skill level, and gamers were always challenged. The goals were attainable, if with difficulty.

Why would anybody ever put up with the old ways of life again? That's what robots were for. Games were satisfaction in its purest, most concentrated and distilled form, and everyone was free to indulge in the drug, or rather the game, of his or her own choice.

In fact, the real world was looked down on, a subject of derision. It was officially ridiculed. Only those abject losers who washed out of game worlds were forced to live in demeaning reality with menial jobs.

Joseph, like almost everyone else, could easily play games the entire day, snacking by the console, not even stopping to eat a full meal or use the bathroom. It was so very hard to stop, but people were only allowed their mandatory four hours of gaming a day unless their profession required additional time. Any more and the intensity of playing led to burnout and rehab.

The authorities generously rewarded game accomplishments. Rewards might mean redeemable tokens, or gaming goods and tools and weapons needed to advance to higher levels, or a better equipped, more attractive and fashionable, higher ranking, higher status, stronger and more skillful, and generally improved avatar. The later was especially effective since, after all, other game players identified each other by their avatars. Starting out with a shabby avatar was disgraceful. Each mission successfully accomplished, each milestone that was met, each new game skill that was acquired, and each new level a player advanced to earned him or her extra tokens. And doing well also meant Humbelixent tablets.

There were also government sponsored halls of fame and rolls of honor players aspired to for each major game.

Joseph combined his game tokens with hazardous duty tokens earned from his work to move up to a larger apartment in a more prestigious neighborhood. It was thus vital to everyone's standard of living to be an accomplished gamer.

Almost everyone was able to earn tokens good for two weeks of vacation per year, time free from having to work. As one of the most successful gamers of his generation and possibly even a future Hall-of-Famer, Joseph amassed enough vacation tokens to spend his two weeks' vacation in the International Virtual World Theme Park. It was a privilege only a handful were able to achieve.

"Hey ElectroWiz481"

"Wat u want?"

"Going 2 Intl Virtual World"

"Wow 4 real!"

"Yep"

"When?"

"End of next month dammit, y they make u wait so long? 6 wks! Can't stand it"

"Patience"

"Y? Earned it. 2 much"

Gamers, that is, everybody, were used to instant satisfaction and immediate feedback.

"Something 2 look forward 2. Chill. Few can go"

"Yeah, cant wait so long"

Chapter Three
South America

Antonia LaFuentes IV was a threatened queen. Never mind that her family had ruled the South American bloc for nearly a century now, passing their iron-clad dictatorial rule down through the family. Her first cousin Augusto was determined to wrest the throne, or rather, the presidency, from her. Her sister Rosa was also had designs on the throne, and plots by other relatives had been nipped in the bud. This kind of family struggle for supremacy was standard and frequently fatal fare. She depended on her top advisor Edwina to be her eyes, ears, and shield.

"Your Most Exalted Highness, I regret to tell you that people are still talking about your brother Hugo's suspicious death," Edwina said. "As you are only too aware he was about to wrest control of the bloc from you when it happened three years ago. People question how he could have suffered a fatal stroke at only twenty-nine years of age. And right now, the only thing holding your sister Rosa in check is that she's afraid of being poisoned herself." They were in LaFuentes's private chambers, a large, lavishly decorated, wood paneled, antique saturated, well-guarded room in the palace interior.

"Nobody can prove anything and the coroner himself died suddenly, so he can't refute his own report. I think people just need something else to occupy their minds. Can't we manufacture another scandal or something?"

"Your Most Merciful and Superior Uniqueness, that's fine for controlling the people but how will you stop your sister and your cousin from plotting against you? Augusto is too ambitious, and if it isn't one cousin it will be another."

LaFuentes was taller than average, not a raving beauty but nevertheless slender, striking, and attractive with her long brown hair and hazel eyes, quite in contrast to her smart but mousy and bespectacled advisor.

"I'm tired of playing whack-a-mole with my relatives. What do you suggest?"

"Your Perfect and Pristine Majesty needs an heir-apparent."

"That won't happen for quite a while. In the meantime, something has to be done to eliminate these moles, I mean threats, permanently, once and for all. I have more important things to do than look over my shoulder all the time. Why can't you discover and prove some hereditary family condition they can succumb to, one that's fatal, one that people will believe?"

"I'll see what I can come up with my Ever Wise and Resourceful Leader. Maybe you need a powerful ally they won't dare cross."

"You mean like Liu? That's a deal with a bushmaster. It's trading one threat for another."

"Your Most Enlightened Rulership, he's just as much of a threat either way, so why not make use of him? Besides, you want to divert people's attention but they don't play games here as much as they do in most of the other blocs."

"That's because we don't have the infrastructure to reach every little village and backwater with the network and it's more difficult to keep track of what people are doing all the time. We can't watch all of their activities 100% of the time and make sure they toe the line."

"What can we do my Far-Seeing All-Knowing Queen? We don't have enough robots or the capital to build out the infrastructure and we don't have enough super-computers to watch everybody."

"That's why I gave Mambler asylum here. I expected him to rebuild his factories in my bloc and produce what we need in exchange for my leniency."

"You mean 'Machete Mike' your Most Ultimate Highness? He's complaining about a lack of factories, a lack of capital, and a lack of construction robots himself."

"I'm tired of his excuses. Let's get rid of him and find someone else."

"Like who, my Very Magnificent Queen of all who are Wise and Good? And besides, he has a point. When Robert Taylor, Jr. took over the Atlantic Alliance Economic Ministry he convicted Mambler of corruption and bribery and confiscated all of his factories in the Atlantic Alliance. He's a fugitive with no ownership there and a price on his head."

"Taylor is pretending to be the first honest politician in the history of the planet. He has to go, too. I can't stand that righteous holier-than-thou act of his. Somebody needs to knock him down a couple of rungs."

"What about Mambler your Most Elevated Royal Highness of Them All? He does still have a few factories here."

"Make it clear he either gets it in gear or he goes to prison for high treason."

"What about magnificus, your Supreme Eminence? They have a superior technology. Maybe we can induce them to help."

"How will I bribe them? I can't sleep with any of them."

"Maybe your Highness can. Maybe you can mate with one of them and produce a few furry goon freaks for your palace guard."

"You're walking on thin ice and I have iron boots."

"What I mean is, they have robot and computer technology that's superior to anyone else's on this planet, my Ultimate Lord and Master. They could catapult you ahead of the other blocs. Find out what they want and make an offer. Get your hands on their technology and you could intimidate and control the other leaders. That's what you really want, isn't it?"

"You know me. Call Mambler. It's time to scare the crap out of him."

"Yes, Madam Queen and President of All That Matters."

Mambler showed up soon thereafter.

"Mambler, I need a lot more production out of you and I want it soon, otherwise I'm sending you back to Taylor, and you know what that will mean."

"I'm doing my best but I need more machinery, more capital, and more robots to make it happen. My factories are straining at full capacity. Can't you get a pardon out of Taylor for me, then I can use my factories there and give you first priority on the output? I want to see that damned Taylor eat crow."

"Same old story. You want more of the robots that you make yourself? Please. I'm the only one who dared to take you in, so you're in no position to give me your excuses. If you can't be of any use to me I'll throw your pathetic self out. I'm going to see if I can work a deal with magnificus to re-engineer your factories, but only if you get your act together. Now get out of here and get to work. I'm watching you."

LaFuentes knew that Edwina was correct, but what bait would she use to enlist magnificus and get the technological edge she wanted? What would magnificus need in return?

* * *

Annie Koler, notorious fugitive computer hacker and weapons expert from Gwydion Prime, sat in her comfortable, stolen orbiting shuttlecraft quarters, eating her favorite pine grass muffins and watching treasured soap opera reruns she brought with her from home. After all, as a stowaway and fugitive, what did she have to lose? She would have been long since dead had she stayed on Gwydion Prime. She was an inter-planetary persona non grata and would never have been invited to join either expedition, so why not fend for herself, and make the most of the situation?

More alarmingly and more importantly, since she had hacked and pilfered the codes for one of magnificus' four lunar-orbiting laser-particle beam weapons, which she took control of as she and her fellow colonists were arriving, Koler expected that control of the weapon would likely prevent the other magnificus from coming after her. Once she sized up the situation, she intended to profit from a bidding war for her weapon services between the most powerful political blocks on Earth. So far, she was able to contact Liu.

Other competing world leaders lost no time contacting her, before she was completely ready for them. They were all aware of the weapon, after she demonstrated it to devastating effect. Koler's demonstration blasted the small island into rubble, evaporating a temporary hole in the atmosphere in the process, which created an extreme low-pressure funnel resulting in a category 5 hurricane, and leaving seriously radioactive residue on the spot. Liu and Earth's other leaders could only marvel in complete awe. And this, she claimed, was low power!

Koler continued trying to hack the other three weapons, which would then be her insurance policy and ace in the hole.

She was offered gourmet food, entertainment packages, and other conveniences delivered to her door, or rather hatch, via special high-priority space drones, as enticements.

* * *

But there was no peace for Annie. To start with, Newman, with the assistance of his staff, had meanwhile identified and quarantined Koler's hack and regained control of the weapon. Worse for her, they had let this be known to Earth's leaders.

Nevertheless, Koler was confident she could find another hack.

And she was growing tired of the incessant badgering and pandering by the Earth's competing leaders. They all wanted her to turn over the weapon or use I on their behalf to squash their rivals and put a final end to this or that supposedly urgent threat, which they all insisted was a threat to her as well.

Now it was that annoying Mitchell pinging her again. What did Liu want this time? OK, lights, action, camera! Be the dutiful insignificant serf in awe of the greatest, most powerful and feared ruler in all of history.

"Hello President Liu. Such an honor for you to summon me. How can I serve you today?"

"Why don't you land your dinky little space toy here. Aren't you tired of your cramped boring monotonous existence? You can live in a huge luxurious villa with dozens of robot servants, and you will want for nothing."

"With all respect to you and your magnanimous offer, no thank you, I don't care to be in anyone's clutches."

"Why are you so insulting today, Koler? I can wipe you out in a minute if I decide to."

"Don't fret, Mr. President. There's safety to consider. I know my place, but even the most despicable rats will scurry for safety."

"What nonsense is it this time?"

"Let me give you an example, Mr. President. We have information that the first anoxygenic photosynthesis in Earth originated more than 3-1/2 billion years ago and was based on molecules like hydrogen sulfide and minerals like arsenic and iron. Carbon dioxide was much more plentiful in the atmosphere then. It used lower energy light more in the red end of the spectrum. This was later displaced by chlorophyll-based systems using more energetic higher frequency light. The point is, those original oxygen producing organisms and their enzymes and chemicals would now be poisonous. With our orange sun, our plants produce oxygen akin to your original anoxygenic organisms, so our plants may well be poisonous to you and your green plants could be poisonous for us. The same considerations apply to our endemic bacteria. So maybe my mere presence is a threat to you."

"You are being ridiculous. The enormous villa I will build for you will have a hermetically sealed bubble, so why do you worry?"

"Mr. President, I'm sure you recognize that my health and whatever value and leverage I have resides up here."

"Look Koler, wouldn't you like to be queen of the Earth?"

"What I really crave, Mr. President, is some new soap operas to watch."

"Alright Koler, if that's your pleasure, I have thousands of actors and writers at my command with cute furry costumes."

"Wright tells me the same thing, Mr. President."

"Why do you always bring *him* up? I forbid you from ever talking to him or mentioning his name again. Just ditch this obsession of yours, Koler. Wright is nothing more than a minor nuisance in the scheme of things. He's nothing. I will squash him like a bug. Why do you always make me remind you I'm the only real power on Earth? Show some respect!"

Just an hour after this call ended, Liu's goon Mitchell contacted her yet again. When would it stop?

"Koler, I'll get right to the point. Carson said you no longer control the weapon, and that its control was distributed among several individuals in their governing council."

"What do you expect him to say? It's a false claim. He has to convince you he has something you want for his own safety and in exchange for allowing him to build his elevator and use your resources for his refueling and maintenance base. Why even bother with Carson's silly wishes? What would you gain? Ignore him and let him rot in space."

"Then how about another demonstration? Directed at your friend Wright."

"You've had your demonstration, Mr. President, and it's not yet time for me to start a war."

These Earthlings were so easy to fool!

* * *

To Carson and magnificus, Annie was a wanted traitor and fugitive.

Newman was still working on a way to hack and take over control of the errant shuttle and bring it and Annie back to the mother ship to face the music. Computer expert versus genius computer hacker. But that was his lowest priority, and it would be quite some time.

* * *

Part of the latest evolving plan was to open secret negotiations with the three biggest power centers and then, if there was progress in the talks, play them off against each other when terms were well in hand and the secret leaked out.

First off was a conference with Martin Wright, president of the Atlantic Alliance.

"Mr. President, I feel I can lay my cards on the table with you," Carson commenced. "I'm sure your spies have told you that Liu is trying to get his hands on our laser-particle beam weapon. What if we moved our entire operation to your territory? Would Liu or anyone else dare attack you when they know we have to defend our assets and we would have to retaliate? How can you support and help insure our success if we do that?"

"Why don't I mobilize our resources and start putting in the necessary infrastructure, so you will see we act in good faith. The leaders of the other blocks are perpetual threats to our territory and independent existence. We will support you if I know your plan will permanently solve my problem. That includes providing me with security. How can I be sure of that?"

"We need an earth base. Our logistics won't support any further travels without it."

"But for how long?"

"Let's get our subordinates together to work out some details and then we shall see."

"The sooner the better. Goodbye."

Just then Newman interrupted Carson, communicator in hand. "I have an audio transmission from someone calling himself Bennigan from the Atlantic Alliance Legislature."

Carson grabbed the device.

"Mr. Carson, I know you are busy and I'm sorry to disturb you, but I wanted to warn you. Can I be sure this conversation is secret and confidential?"

"I can assure you it is."

"As Chairman of the Legislature, Martin Wright is only our acting president until the legislature elects a new president and vice president, but that will never happen. Wright has the power to block all nominations, so he may as well be dictator for life. I'm telling you, he is a slippery character. Always ask yourself what he might be doing behind your back."

"Thank you for letting me know. And what do you want in return for this information?"

"Nothing. Just your secrecy and my job. I have to always watch *my* own back with Wright. I do have a suggestion that will benefit both of us."

Here comes the punch line Carson thought. "What is it?"

"Get Wright to establish a joint study and research center to nail down the details of a possible agreement. I'm in a position to present it to him. I will also suggest I be appointed director. Since I am one of his rivals in the legislature, it's an opportunity for him to get me out of the way, and safer for me, too. You need humans to explain our motives and actions to you. We could have secret connection under cover of the official correspondence, but it has to be secure or I am toast. We can try to surmise what is really going on behind the scenes. It will help both of us in a strategic way."

Carson was trying to figure out Bennigan's real motive and what he was up to, but overall, a large-scale joint effort had a lot to offer. "I agree and we need to move on this ASAP. I will present the case to Wright immediately and make the strongest case I can. You can then say 'me, too', and push from your end. If I move first that gives you some cover."

"Agreed."

But just who was this Bennigan? Surveillance demonstrated that John Bennigan was vice-chairman of the legislature and one of Wright's long-time rivals.

Interesting development, but was it trustworthy? Magnificus had wanted to believe they could trust and rely on Wright. Maybe it was time for Plan C.

"I think we should suggest to all of the blocs that they set up a research center we could potentially participate in for each of their territories," suggested Lewis. "We don't want to appear to be showing favoritism towards anyone. They could see that as a provocation, especially Liu. Whether any of the blocs agree is up to them. If any do set up a center, whether we participate in their research should depend on the progress of further negotiations."

"Good suggestion, I agree," said Carson. "Since Liu wants us to talk to him alone, I expect he will take offense anyway."

That meant it was time for a conversation with Queen LaFuentes. Or rather, with her chief advisor Edwina.

"Her Glorious Majesty doesn't have the time to waste on the likes of you, but we can still be of great assistance. I am available to discuss it with you," Edwina told Carson.

"Then you are aware we want to establish a refurbishing and refueling base there, and I would like your support on that. We have to construct two dual space elevators at equatorial locations, and we need your resources along with manufacturing that we will supply ourselves. In return we can assist you with some of our advanced technology. We want to reassure you that we have no desire to take over or rule Earth. Are you willing to help us, and what do you want in return?"

"I'm sure we can come to a mutually beneficial arrangement I can present to her Exalted Eminence. But you must be aware that you are still a threat to Earth's people whether you intend it or not."

"How is that?"

"Many people depend on the status quo. Cheaters, thieves, the corrupters and corrupted, the rent seekers, the skimmers and bribers and officials on the take, and all of the other parasites who prey on the system and its people, they all expect to be enriched by things as they are. Many other people are comfortable with it because it is what they know. All of them will fight against change. New knowledge, new ways of doing things, and new customs automatically bring change. Once people know something new, they can't be forced to not know. You threaten all of these people. There are opportunists who will welcome the new knowledge and customs you represent, but I warn you, those are few and far between. Just by coming here, you make many enemies you aren't even aware of."

"I see. I am at a temporary loss to respond to that," Carson told Edwina.

"Be aware that if you want to be successful you need to work out a source of income. No matter where you go, you will have a lot of palms to grease if you don't want sabotage."

"Thank you for the advice."

"First, there's a place for your elevators. Africa and South America are your most likely choices. I can tell you right now there aren't many stable locales on the equator in Africa that have the infrastructure to build what you want. You would have to contract to create it. How will you pay or trade for this work? I think your best bet is here in South America. Parts of Brazil, Columbia, and Ecuador fall along the equator. There might be something near Quito or in the Galapagos Islands near major roads or shipping lanes.

"Let me be frank," Edwina continued. "Since our technology entrepreneur and guru Michael Mambler fled our territory for North

America, and the government there took over his plants, his robotics, computer and game factories in South America are floundering. He was our most important supplier, especially after he bribed former Alliance President Swift and his crony officials into giving him sole source contracts. Then he became a wanted criminal in the Atlantic Alliance as well. We allowed him to return here, so we want you to assist us with upgrading and running his factories and improving the technology, especially the robots and supercomputers."

"I suggest we have our staffs talk further and see what we can work out," Carson replied. Here at least, might be the beginning of a deal.

Later, Newman opined to Carson that "No one bloc has or wants to provide everything we want. And, as we've often said, we need cooperation or acquiescence from all of the major powers. Should we undertake three-way negotiations?"

"Two-way is difficult enough. Now how do we deal with Liu? At least he makes no bones about what he wants, including an exclusive deal."

"I know, he will agree to anything but adhere to nothing. How do we hold his feet to the fire?" Newman asked.

"He will only talk if he gets a weapon, but that doesn't mean he will carry out his end of the bargain."

"Do you think we can satisfy him by offering the most advanced technology of anybody? Then he can dominate with it if he wants to, and the rest is up to him."

"Too dangerous." Carson said. "Guess what he will do with the technology."

"Do you think we can put the fear into him that one of his rivals will get the weapon instead of him? Maybe he will panic and maybe agree to serious negotiations for once."

"That would probably be a declaration of war in his eyes. I think maybe we should ignore Liu. Let his spies discover our other negotiations. He'll be totally irate and make a mistake. He should want to reach a deal and try to exclude the others. In the meantime, we can answer his calls and be polite."

"Or he could try to solve the problem by eradicating us," Newman offered.

"But that won't get him his weapon. You think he is entirely rational? I don't. Besides, if he doesn't get a weapon he will be perpetually plotting to get his hands on it by any underhanded means he can conjure up."

"Who can we trust and for how long? Won't we have to leave a weapon here to protect our base anyway, along with staff we can't spare to look after it?"

"So, what do you suggest we do?" Carson solicited.

"Leave Liu out of it for now. Let's start with that until somebody comes up with something better."

"What if we do reach an agreement and make a treaty with Liu? He will ignore any parts of it that interfere with his ambitions."

"I suggest making a detailed schedule part of every agreement or treaty," Newman said. "The deal is off if there are any slippages however minor."

Suddenly, a speaker called on Liu's channel, interrupting the conversation. "Hello Mr. Carson. This is Sam Darling from 'Today's Entertainment'. You know, the people of Earth are so curious and want to know much more about you and why you are here. They want their doubts and fears about you soothed. This is your big chance for some good publicity, for you to establish a bond with the people of Earth, to gain their trust and get help with your aims. Rumors are everywhere, and I can offer you a chance to set them straight. It's your golden opportunity. You can't turn it down."

"How did you happen to break into this conversation?"

"We are media people. We understand networks and systems."

"Do you mind letting me conclude my other business?"

"Sure, but think about my offer and we will be in touch again."

"What was that all about?" Carson asked Dr. Holland who was floating nearby.

"Sounds to me like a ploy by Liu. He wants to gather data about you and everyone else here, estimate our strength and the limits of our technology, and any other information he can use against us."

"What do you suggest we do then?"

"Would a little disinformation campaign help us along?"

"I don't see how."

"Well, just an idea."

"You can think about it and make your case."

* * *

Gwydion Prime had had an active space exploration program using huge space-borne telescopes and interstellar probes. The search for new habitable planets was the focus. Everybody knew time was running out. In order to transmit and receive radio broadcasts from its interstellar probes, magnificus had remodeled an asteroid to act as a relay station. A two-and-a-half-mile parabolic depression was blasted out of a 3-mile wide asteroid and fitted with a fine mesh antenna surface and a receiver at the focal point. The rest of the asteroid was also carved away to make it as light as possible. Gyroscopes and attitude control jets were fitted for pointing accuracy, as were an array of solar panels, a small antenna to retransmit signals to Gwydion Prime, and refillable fuel tanks with a capacity of twenty-five earth years for the jets. A similar large relay antenna near Earth was vital, but since Carson and his crew had no possibility of using a near-earth asteroid in the foreseeable future, they had to find another option. Arecibo, the collapsed and dilapidated concave hole in the ground that once served as the world's largest radio-telescope, was a possibility, faster than building from scratch. Yet Arecibo was small compared to the asteroid antenna magnificus once possessed, and it would not be that effective. Special measures would be necessary to compensate, including slowing the transmission rate to a crawl while using the probes' full power, adding extra error correction coding, transmitting the most vital and compact information first while leaving photographs and other high bandwidth information until last, and using state-of-the-art electronics. Even then, it was likely that some probes would run out of power long before everything was sent. And retransmission would be just as slow as reception.

When a probe reached another star system, the initial communication was via "twangles," that is, entangled electrons. Each probe carried a painstakingly protected complement of 4800 of these entangled electrons with the matching and equally protected set back on Gwydion Prime. After analysis of the target solar system, each probe returned two identical 1200-bit (150 character) coded twanglets, the so-called twangles, instantly delivered via half of the precious entangled electrons. Coded digits indicated if any promising planets or moons existed, location in the habitable zone, how likely it was they were habitable, and the estimated degree and risk of terraforming them. A duplicate twangle sent from Gwydion Prime gave the probe the spherical coordinates to use for transmitting its observations, the power level and transmission rate, and a periodic transmission schedule, although these radio frequency messages from the probe would not be received for decades. Galacticus magnificus brought entangled electron sets with them to Earth, carefully stabilized and preserved.

Twanglets worked as if you detached both your thumb and forefinger from your hand and banished them to opposite ends of the galaxy. They are no longer attached to your hand and have no physical connection to each other. A vast space, a gulf of, for example, a hundred to a hundred and fifty thousand light years, or more than six hundred thousand trillion miles, might separate them along with a huge expanse of time, more than a hundred thousand years. Yet you can still pinch them together in an instant, and each one will immediately feel the pinch of the other, as if they were still a single entity attached to your hand. The phenomenon seems to completely defy all experience and common sense. It is a clue that space and time are not fundamental. What is the mysterious secret, the hidden true structure, of space and time that there can be so much separation between your thumb and forefinger (or two entangled particles) but yet no space at all? It was still an unsolved mystery.

Large telescopes orbited both Gwydion Prime and at its Lagrange points. Large near-infrared and visible light coronagraph equipped telescopes hunted for suitable rocky planets in the habitable zones of late F, G, and early K-type stars in any orbital inclination, not just the 4% of exoplanets that eclipse their host stars. These telescopes also looked for planet-sized moons orbiting larger planets in stable orbits around quiet middle-aged M-dwarfs, although moons were much more difficult to detect. Other orbiting telescopes were able to take long exposure spectrographs and attempt to determine the atmospheric composition and to measure the magnetosphere of candidate planets. This exploration concentrated on planets less than a hundred and sixty light years away, the estimated outer survivable limit astronauts could travel before their DNA was irreversibly scrambled by high energy charged particles, that is, cosmic rays, and gamma rays. A series of probes were planned to the most promising planets and moons, but only a fraction was ever launched.

There was no possibility magnificus could duplicate this effort from Earth in the next century or two. For the time being they had to rely on data already collected and probes previously launched from Gwydion Prime.

* * *

How long had magnificus been trapped in their sterile, confined quarters, soaring through interstellar space with no comfortable, hospitable home planet to settle on?

"This is no life, dear," Forbes complained to Jaspar. "We haven't been able to settle into any kind of a routine since we've been here. Things are only bearable during hibernation."

They were in their small plain compartment, the walls full of pictures of their former friends and family on their now-uninhabitable home planet.

"I know. We still have no home and these earthlings are a troublesome lot."

"Time to go join the others in the conference room for a status briefing."

Along the way, they paused to gaze at the Earth together through one of the few portholes.

The lit portion of Earth was bathed in the yellow-white light of its Sun. John and Renee longed for home and wondered what it would be like to live on this planet, to experience first-hand the yellow-green forests, the white clouds suspended from the heavens in a nearly invisible sky, pale greenish oceans covering more than two-thirds of the planet, brown deserts. With their eyes having evolved to see the less intense orange hew of their home star, they saw near infrared up through yellow-green colors, but were not sensitive to blue or blue-green. Earth's plants were a mesmerizing contrast to the orange-red hue of the plants on Gwydion Prime, with its oceans covering three-quarters of it surface, but otherwise both planets were similar.

John asked, "I wonder what our destination planet will look like? It has a K3 star, only a little cooler and redder than our own. I think we will like it there."

"I hope so. Let's go now. We don't want to make Carlson wait."

"Reports?" Carlson asked.

Jaspar started it off. "I've been looking at the South American proposal and the only locations readily accessible by sea, air, or highway are La Mitad del Mundo near Quito Ecuador, Macapá at the northern mouth of the Amazon in Brazil, and Isabela Island in the Galapagos Islands," Taylor told Carson.

"Being from a cooler planet, the heat is too intense for us on Earth's equator except for short stays. The space elevator will have to be automated, staffed, and defended by robots. I think Galapagos would be my first choice. It's isolated for security, and that's important. It's also accessible by sea for shipping large components. La Mitad del Mundo is my second choice."

"It's likely the other blocs will want to capture or at least control the space elevator so they can take it over and use it for their military and espionage launches. We could rent it to them equally for peaceful purposes, but I recommend assembling a multi-bloc automated defense force with equal representation from every bloc to defend it."

"And Queen LaFuentes is onboard with this?"

"According to Edwina."

"Our communications with them are encrypted?"

"Always."

"Have you worked out what we will provide in return?"

"Their greatest need is for more robots and more and better computers. That will keep them interested. We both need income so we have several joint ventures in mind."

"Can all of it be automated and run entirely by robots when we leave?"

"That's problematic. I hope it is a matter of system design."

"What about the Atlantic Alliance?"

"Negotiations are going slowly. Their number one interest is in having us protect them from the other blocs, or obtaining a weapon from us for that purpose. They want absolute and eternal protection. Naturally we don't want to get involved in foreign politics and power struggles, nor do we want to be obligated to station a permanent peace keeping force on this outpost. They are dragging their feet until they get our guarantee, and we are looking for a solution and a way to break that impasse."

"What about Liu?"

"He still demands immediate ownership of a weapon, but we've intercepted his communications with Annie and know that he also wants to get his hands on her shuttle, the equipment in it, and whatever else of ours he can grab so he can reverse engineer them. I don't see this as a carrot we can safely dangle in front of him," Newman summarized.

"Does he know about our other negotiations?"

"I get the distinct impression he does and he's holding his fire."

"Then there's no way of avoiding trouble now. It still bothers me that Earth isn't what I expected from the data our probes sent back to us," Carlson complained. "It's just different."

"To be expected," replied Forbes. "The probe's transmissions took decades to get from Earth to our planet and we took ten times that to travel to the Earth. It would be suspicious if Earth hadn't changed in the meantime."

Chapter Four
A Wedding

"mom, will u come 2 my wedding, pls? I would really like it if u do"

"then y don't u have virtual wedding like every1 else? I wont allow any daughter of mine 2 go real. U know the saying, 'Go real, go rogue.' it's true, there's a reason y. now just snap out of it. real never lasts"

"dad promised 2 b there. pls"

"chattertwitted him, sure he will. u have him twisted round ur little finger. I told him not 2 fall 4 it"

"he wants 2 b there"

"you know u and ur husband cant live together anyway only ur avatars"

"same thing"

Megan's Chattertwits were to no avail.

The wedding was already planned. Two more weeks. It would, of course, be a simple affair before the robot magistrate, the Justice of the Pieces, since real meetings were heavily discouraged among the common people. Only immediate family would be allowed to attend, and nearly all of them would be avatars.

"daddy I'm scared. wat if he runs when he sees me? wat if he doesnt like the real me? nobody knows who I really am. only u"

"then I will tell him wat a great daughter u are. I think u should change to virtual. do u think it's worth the risk?"

"dunno but he doesn't want virtual. he's not like everybody else"

"does he have anyone coming?"

"his mother avatar will come from Vancouver. father died 2 yrs ago"

"wat does she think? does she approve?"

"dunno"

* * *

It was now ten o'clock. The wedding was an hour away. They were gathered in the plain, light-blue walled, windowless underground waiting room next to the chapel entrance. Joseph and Megan arrived first.

It had been twenty years since Megan had seen her father in person, when she was a year old. Of course, she had no conscious memory of it, but she still recognized him with an electric jolt the instant he entered the room. They instinctively hugged each other despite the impropriety of doing so.

"Hi sweetheart, if everything falls apart it's worth it to see you again after so many years."

"For me, too."

"Did your mother change her mind? You two have a lot in common, same profession."

"She won't be here. She doesn't approve of this."

"Are you ready to meet your fiancé before you go through with it?"

"I can't stand it. I think I'm going to faint."

"Make it quick. That must be him coming right now."

"Oh my God!" she gasped." You look just like your Mugbook pictures!" she said to him. "Nobody dares to do that. Why didn't you Imageshop them? Are you some kind of pervert or something? Nobody puts their real photos out there. What's wrong with you?"

"My way of hiding in plain sight, I guess. You must be Megan. You don't look anything like your avatar."

Megan's face fell instantly. Unlike her smooth complected, blue-eyed online pictures, she had a somewhat broken skin and brown eyes but was nonetheless attractive in her own way.

"You look better," Ben Richards continued.

"Dr. Richards, let me introduce myself," Joseph said as he extended his right hand. "I'm Megan's father Joseph."

"Very pleased to meet you. Didn't expect you in person."

"Megan tells me you're working on a new video game. When will it be available? I'd like to try it."

"I'm creating it as a hobby. The government hasn't approved it yet and I don't know that they ever will."

"Then why are you bothering with it? Why wouldn't they approve it?"

"It's a space wars kind of game. You know the government doesn't want people to bother themselves with space exploration, travel, the environment, economic issues, or anything external. They only want self-absorbed games or games that feature the politicians as heroes. I doubt they would ever license a game like mine."

"Shhh! be quiet then. You never know when some robot is listening."

"I do hope that one day I'll be able to convince the authorities it's worthwhile. I can make Liu or Wright the heroic leader of the galaxy and all of the other politicians are villains. They would like that sort of thing."

"Just don't release it underground. I don't want my daughter marrying a felon."

"Don't worry. I'll take good care of her. I won't distribute the game without approval."

"She tells me you're a happiness engineer. Doesn't that take a lot of schooling?"

"Yes, but I prefer the official title 'neurochemical engineer'."

"Sure. Why don't the two of you talk and get acquainted before you go through with this?"

"My intent exactly. I've never met the real Megan, though I don't know how well I can get to know her in only five or ten minutes. You know, with social media you always have to try and read between the lines. This is speed dating on steroids."

The main room was attractive enough, like a toned-down Las Vegas marriage chapel, with fake gothic windows with white chiffon draperies, patterned red wall paper, hardwood floors, and a smallish wooden platform in the back. As legally required, it was a ten-minute civil ceremony; a best robot, a robot-of-honor and piped-in music of the bride's choosing were provided. No game points were awarded.

The wedding party was unable to rent a rice throwing machine to use at the conclusion of the ceremony. Instead, afterwards, the four of them planned their own private family "reception." Their avatars took a picnic lunch to a simulated public park. Like most such parks, it was modelled after a real deserted and run-down park, complete with tall grass, rotting picnic tables, litter, and lots of rodents. If any real parks remained, they would have been long since abandoned. No matter, everything was available online and could hardly be distinguished from the real thing anyway.

"There's a mossy spot over there. Not much tall grass to walk through. We can spread out the blanket and eat," Ben's mother said.

"Do you like the sandwiches?" Megan asked. "I just printed them this morning, especially for this occasion."

"Thank you but I'm not happy about your real wedding and I don't have an appetite right now," Joseph replied.

"Thank heaven none of you mentioned this on Mugbook," Joseph said to Ben's mother. "It would be so embarrassing."

"Seems that nobody knows about it. Ben tells me you're a high voltage electrician."

"Yeah. Plenty of bonus tokens. How about you?"

"Robot doctor assistant, two hours a day."

"That means you're in contact with people face-to-face."

"Don't know. Still can't tell what's real and what's avatar. None of my Mugbook or Chattertwit friends ever recognize me. Guess I don't look or sound much like my online appearance."

"Tell me, Megan, do you have a baby license?"

"Not yet. They're so hard to get."

"What will you do for your next twenty or thirty minutes together?"

"Not much we can do. Can't get tickets or extended time to a reality park so we'll just hang out here, maybe walk around a bit."

"Aren't you going to play games together? You can be a team, earn some tokens together. Even if it's just virtual."

"Maybe we'll give it a try. I think we should do something else for a change, special occasion and all."

"My advice is to make the most of this."

"We will. Dear, I don't think you and your mother know what a success my father is. He's in the gamer's honor roll and the Holy Race winner's circle, and he's being recognized with a trip to International Virtual World."

"That's wonderful," Ben's mother said. "The top winners there get so many tokens they move up to big apartments in celebrity neighborhoods, they have lots of personal robot assistants. Some of them even become A-listers and get to Chattertwit with the stars. You never even hear of some of the players after they go there. After their trip to a virtual park, they just disappear somewhere."

"Yeah, I think some of them win so much they climb way up the ladder and from then on they only converse in private with other celebrities from some exclusive new neighborhood."

"I once heard that one or two of the top A-listers were even granted sky lights so they could see what above ground looks like."

"I'm sure that's just another lying meme. They tell you the ultraviolet outside will kill you."

"Skylight or not, I do hope you're successful there, but you won't forget the rest of us, will you?"

"Never."

"It will be hard to say goodbye now that we've all been together like this."

"I know but our time is up," Joseph said. "It's been great to meet you. Maybe we'll find a way to do it again one day."

* * *

"Shouldn't we be playing games now?" The two of them were in Richards' modest apartment.

"You can login and play. Since I know from my work what games are good for, the only game I play is the one I'm working on."

"But you could be arrested for not playing sanctioned games for your required four hours a day."

"Oh, don't worry about that. I programmed a bot to play for me, that way I have more time for my research. As far as the government knows I'm as addicted as everyone else."

"You only hinted to me what you do. Nobody knows what a 'happiness engineer' does, or as you want to be called, a 'neurochemical engineer'. What are you hiding?"

"Nothing. As you well know, the government has to license all games and they dictate changes their creators have to make before the public can play. Those changes are based on testing and work by people like me. Playing games invokes emotional and neurochemical reactions, and it's my responsibility to make sure those reactions are the ones the state wants, at least for the games they assign to me. Game testers, like what your brother wants to be, are really guinea pigs. We use them to see if we're pulling the right emotional strings."

"What is it you try to do?"

"First, people have to be uncontrollably addicted to the games. The government wants it to be exactly like a drug addiction but without the bad side effects. People build up a physiological tolerance to drugs so the dosage has to keep increasing. The heavy doses disable people and destroy their motivation and capacity for productive work, not to mention eroding their morals. Eventually there is total burnout. That's not acceptable. It's the same with rich unhealthy food, gambling, and other addictions. They all become destructive. People end up enslaved by their addiction and will do anything to get their hands on their drug of choice.

"The slick thing about games is, you can create the addiction, the craving, and the insatiable need without the adverse side effects. If people do what you want, they get points they can use to advance in their games. If they do well in their games, they can get tokens to exchange for daily necessities. Instead of robbing and looting to get money to buy the drugs they crave and can't live without, people play games and do your bidding. It's a lot like training a dog.

"We accomplish all that by manipulating people's neurochemical response to the games. The ultimate goal is a docile, easily managed, easily manipulated population, one the authorities can play like a well-tuned fiddle."

"I think I just married a monster. Do I really want to know how you do it?"

"Don't worry about me, but you ought to know what you're up against.

"First of all, games can activate reward pathways in the brain by facilitating the release of dopamine. This can be magnified with the release of noradrenaline and serotonin. These can be triggered by providing a sense of pride and satisfaction in game accomplishments, and by maintaining a state of intense concentration and a high degree of arousal. Keeping the game level at the very edge of the player's capability, and providing intermittent rewards along with the disappointment of just missing the attainment of goals, promotes this concentration and high arousal. Continual feedback keeps the player hooked and prevents mental lapses that might allow the player to divert his attention to something else.

"Oxytocin and vasopressin are chemicals with a wide range of effects. They can give a sense not only of reward and reinforcement, but of bliss and ecstasy. These chemicals are also associated with sexual cravings and that's why manipulating their release and subsequent suppression through virtual sex games is so useful to the state. Oxytocin can also help prevent the build-up of long-term tolerance to opiates. It is especially released through group interaction and makes social camaraderie rewarding. Games have to be designed to stimulate the release of these neurochemicals. That's why games emphasize alliances and group action. That's why there are mandatory players' social groups for every game, and it's why everyone is indoctrinated from an early age so that their loyalties are to gaming groups, not to their family or relatives.

"Games are also meant to stimulate the Vegas nerve through their realism, by simulating live action. That helps to involve the player in the action just like a high-energy live performance can do. When a game dilemma or crisis arrives, the player will feel 'choked up' and not be able to turn his attention away to anything else.

"Games have to maximize ambiguous clues and stimuli, and unanchored sensual experience, and require players to make quick decisions based on these incomplete clues. That heightens the gamers' concentration and induces a curiosity that releases endorphins, particularly beta endorphin which is eighty times more powerful than morphine and even more addictive.

"My job is to redesign games assigned to me to take fullest possible advantage of these neurochemical pathways.

"When I'm finished with my work, the game psychologists take over and insert subtle propaganda messages and associations into the games.

"So now you can see why games are so effective at spoon feeding education, but the problem there is that students don't come to value knowledge for its own sake but for the rewards of the learning games. They don't develop any desire to expand their field of knowledge or to obtain the benefits of that knowledge.

"You might have noticed that they really do increase the dosages as part of the games but in the gaming world it's called 'leveling up'.

"So, you see, I'm a whore of the state."

"Me, too. Don't forget I'm a Computer Applications Director. I recommend what kinds of games should be made available to people based on government guidelines and my feel for what people will be drawn to, then look for specific games to finalize and test. Now I'm afraid you just taught me where those guidelines come from. Don't you feel dirty? I do because of what you just explained."

"More than you realize. The government assigned me to my profession. It's not the one I would have chosen."

"I don't understand, why are you inventing a new game if you don't approve of them?"

"It's a game that can guide players in a new direction and stimulate their interest in the outside world. In other words, it's totally subversive."

"Show me your new game. What's it about?"

"It's a shooter game. Interplanetary war, but the weapons aren't guns and lasers, although there is *some* of that."

"What are you doing now?"

"I'm playing against the computer. To even out the field I always assign the computer to start at the lowest level. You start from your own home planet with fleets of interplanetary ships of different kinds that you have to defend. At first your home planet is in a neighborhood with lots of other imperialistic planets, and you only have one small fleet with one of each kind of ship. You have to complete some minor missions to get points to buy more ships, weapons, tools, biological agents, bombs, and whatnot. You decide what you need based on your strategy and defensive needs. Early on you have to forge alliances or else you're toast. That's the level I start the computer at, level zero. When you advance to higher levels you can migrate to another planet in a more strategic galactic neighborhood and you can have better ships, weapons, tools, and technology. When I play, I start at one of the advanced levels but the computer still beats me most of the time."

Roar! Ben launched two surveillance craft towards Compu-planet, his one and only rival in this game. Next, he took his snow machine to the top of Mt. Virtual and trained his large telescope on the planet to try and find out what was going on. Was there the tell-tale gleam of a newly launched rocket? Were there any explosions? Was the spectral data normal or did it indicate something untoward? Were there any catastrophes pending on Compu-planet so that the civilization had no choice except to conquer his own home planet? The return information from the surveillance rockets and the telescope only comes back at the speed of light, so it could take years and be out of date. Therefore, he had to anticipate.

Suddenly, boom! A skirmish cruiser from Compu-planet took out his telescope sensor with a laser beam. "Damn it, now I'm blind.

"My defensive sensor was deployed on the other side of my planet. That's the direction I expected an attack to come from. There has to be a surveillance probe orbiting somewhere. The computer must have had its fleet previously deployed and scattered between nearby planets already. That means Compu-planet is undefended. Now it's a race to see if I can get my attack fleet there before the computer can recall its other ships."

"Configuring… configuring…" the game voice repeated.

"Configure for minimum bomb load and maximum speed," Ben told the gaming system. "Program to attack the heart of the Compu-planet's infrastructure. Ignore defenses. Suicide mission if necessary, but hold back two battleships in reserve. Go for the kill at all costs."

"What are you doing?"

"Going for broke. I'm gambling by only keeping one defensive cruiser around my own planet, and holding two battleships in reserve in the attack fleet. Instead of withdrawing its fleet to defend its home planet, the computer could gamble and send everything here and try to overwhelm my defenses. Then it's a race to see if I can get to Compu-planet before that fleet arrives here, but I don't know where the computer's ships were pre-deployed, so I don't know who will win. I'll try to render Compu-planet uninhabitable for the computer. That means destroying all of the computer's power sources. I expect the computer to try to do the same to me, maybe poisoning the water or spreading disease spores. I'm reducing my bomb load to save weight and maximize my ships' speed."

Boom! Crash! Flashes of light! Laser fire, bombs, and explosions rocked both planets, leaving both crippled but still barely habitable. Ben's defensive cruiser was still flying but badly mauled. The computer was left with just two light cruisers while Ben was left with two battleships and a freighter for a second attack wave on Compu-planet.

"What will you do now?" Megan asked.

"Look for another planet to move to. The computer will look for a planet with hydro or geothermal power sources on dry land and with temperatures that won't freeze or fry its electronics. I will look for a new planet with land, liquid water, food sources, and a reasonable climate. If planets aren't available, we have to terraform one."

"What do you think the computer will do?"

"It will disguise what it's doing, but both of us will try to sabotage the other's move and terraforming efforts."

"Don't your time frames have to be compressed? Those moves would take decades or centuries in real life."

"Yes, it's all compressed. A century can happen in an hour or even a couple of minutes."

"How many players could there be in a real game?"

"Hundreds. In a real game with many players, I would be mostly defenseless unless I worked with carefully chosen strategic allies. That would also help get me promoted to a higher level. I would use different subterfuges, like introducing nukes or weaponized germs to a civilization that's too primitive to refrain from using them on itself, because rival political blocs on the planet may seize on any weapon with an immediate benefit, regardless of the longer-term consequences."

"Couldn't that backfire? If they make their planet uninhabitable you couldn't use it either."

"It could, or they could be more advanced than I thought and turn around and use the weapons on *me*."

"How about using particle beam weapons on them?"

"That would slow them down if they didn't capture the weapons to use themselves. Another way is to send research ships protected by fighters. I could try to find biological agents that are lethal to the other planet's higher life forms without disrupting any critical eco-systems and that aren't harmful to me or anything on my own home planet. Other players can also try to do the same to me. A safer way is to intentionally nudge a comet in a planet's Oort cloud and send it inward to cause a mass extinction. You can do that from a distance, undetected. You have to have defenses ready for things like that yourself. In a two-player game the computer could win that way, but the disadvantage is that my planet becomes uninhabitable for a while and the computer can't take it over for a long time and it can't level up."

"There's an awful lot of delays getting information and a lot of educated guess work."

"Mainly because information travels at the speed of light and could take months or years to gather. The situation could have changed significantly by the time you gather your intelligence. Of course, game time is compressed and these things can happen fast."

"You have too many strategic factors. It takes a graduate degree to play your game."

"There are simpler modes with fewer variables for players who aren't up to the full game. One of the modes assumes that light and data travels at infinite speeds."

"You still have to play the probabilities. You will be wrong sometimes."

"Just like Las Vegas and gambling games. You have to work the probabilities in your favor and you can't risk a catastrophic loss that will put you out of the game or reduce you back to newbie status. Some people like gambling versions."

"How do you get your points and tokens?"

"Two ways. First, you can destroy the other civilizations and then take over their planets, not by shooting them or bombing them, but by inducing them to destroy themselves. For example, you can show them how to build nukes when their sense of social responsibility is too weak to restrain them from using the weapons on themselves. Another way is to give them environmentally toxic ways to make money in the short term while destroying their habitat in the longer term. My game rewards taking a long view. Every other game I know of gives immediate feedback and immediate rewards. Like a lot of real life, a short-term strategy can gain the player temporary points but then these points and more are forfeit by long term adverse consequences.

"Another way to win and get points is to destroy an opponent's economic system so they can't afford to stop you from moving in. There are a few other lines of approach to conquer an inhabited planet, for example, taking advantage of peculiarities in their political power structure or their instincts and the peculiarities of their social inhibitions. Instincts vary by planet and depend on planet resources and climate, geologic and social histories, solar and space weather and extinction events, and other factors. Only the highest levels of game plays make this information available and allows you to use it. Another limitation is the assumption that there is only one intelligent species per planet, and if there were any competing intelligences, genocide wiped them out."

"What if the inhabitants intentionally render their planet uninhabitable, like a scorched earth policy?"

"They lose points. You either have to wait for the planet to naturally recover, plan a reclamation project, or re-terraform it. You get points for that but only when you are successful, not right away."

"Who will play your game if they can't get instant gratification? People will always go for the short-term gain. That's all they've ever known. It's all they are allowed to know."

"Then they won't get to the highest levels."

"Nobody is going to play that kind of game."

"Only a rare few, especially since it has to be an underground game the authorities will try to stamp out. If I make it available, I hope that over time, people will learn to prefer it."

"Isn't there a faster way to conquer another planet?"

"You can spin them."

"How?"

"Be clever and cunning, figure out their instincts, their culture, what the people want, and what the authorities want them to have. Tell the authorities you will help them dominate the planet. Convince the people you will give them what they think they want if they let you take over. Nobody passes up an offer for free booty with no effort expended on their part. If you do it right, they will willingly give you the keys to the planet. When you gain control, forget your promises and propaganda and do whatever you want to."

"That sounds uncomfortably familiar not to mention unethical. Is there another way?"

"You can overawe or intimidate them. If the planet is primitive, you can dazzle them with your superiority. You can pretend you're one of their gods, or you can show them your overwhelming firepower and convince them you will destroy them and takeover anyway, so why don't they make a mutually advantageous deal? Offer them life in prison and commute the death penalty. That one only works if they think you hold all the high cards. If not, you can try to bluff them, give them a magic show, flim-flam them with the Wizard of Oz treatment. Nothing to lose by trying except your credibility."

"Anything else?"

"It can be a great advantage to make a deal with the leadership of another planet and form an alliance. All alliances are temporary, though, strictly a matter of expediency. You can also find an uninhabited or formerly inhabited planet and terraform it. Terraforming is complicated and isn't always successful, and it can result in runaway effects and environmental disaster. It also takes a long time."

"So, you really intend it to be a multi-player game?"

"Absolutely. You compete with other players to take over planets and ultimately the galaxy, but you can also form alliances. You have to watch your back, though. If an alliance takes over a planet, you have to find a way to double-cross your partners and wipe them out or squeeze them out, then seize the planet for yourself alone."

"There are so many games to pick from already I don't see the point of one more, even if it's different somehow."

"It's all navel gazing. I want people to look up, see the big picture. There's an outside chance it could be accepted if I make the president of a bloc the universal omnipotent grand poohbah of the universe and the ultimate alpha male, and the rulers of other planets become evil political rivals."

"The authorities will squash your game and maybe you with it if you aren't careful. It would have to be an underground game but then if they catch you, they'll lock you up for life or use you for their medical experiments."

"We'll see. I have a plan. Megan, are you satisfied with the kind of life we're forced to lead? I always sensed you weren't."

"It doesn't matter. We have no choice but to make the most of what we have. What about you?"

"I want to know what else is out there, what other kinds of lives are possible. Nowadays nobody cares about anything unless it's a made-up part of a virtual world."

"Don't complain. The real world is nothing but unrewarding drudgery."

"Are you so sure? Since magnificus came here, we know there's someone else out there. We know there are other goals worth pursuing."

"Then send your game to magnificus. You seem to think that gaming and social intercourse are merely distractions of the modern world."

"Worse than that. The real world is denigrated. It's the new Gnosticism. Games are spirit, the real world is carnal evil. I want to find a way to change that attitude."

"Good luck, Don Quixote."

Chapter Five
The Agreement

"Im tired of being the puppeteer. cant stand myself. dont u feel sleazy 2?"

Richards texted his wife from his apartment. She had long since returned to her own place.

"i try not 2 think bout wat I'm doing. don't think u should either"

"stuck in this life. we're not like everyone else, u know. we measure the real effect of gaming worlds. both of us have 1 ft in real world and 1 ft in virtual. i question what Im doing and y. dont u?" Richards texted his wife on his way home from his morning work at a lab. Texting was still the most natural way to have a conversation.

"no choice. put ur mind on something else"

"dont want this anymore. want something diff"

"like what? pls lets b satisfied with what we have, good jobs, big perks and tokens, 20 hour work week, games every day. y u torture yourself?"

"mind won't sleep. we cant hide from reality. cant b virtual 24 7"

"distract urself. u can if u try. y cant u just put urself on a different plane?"

"coz i know it's all a neurochemical trick and Im 1 of the tricksters"

"i understand ur skepticism."

"feel 2 confined. want 2 escape. gaming world builds and flatters ego but crushes my soul. alternate realities let me project my faults and fears onto the game figures but then i forget who i am. a devil's bargain"

"try 2 go with it. besides, wat would u replace it with?"

"want to understand wat the universe and my place in it like magnificus. not liv in a fantasy"

"you'll go up in flames if they catch u talking like that. better stop it"

"another thing, dear. i want 2 b together, really together. cyber only doesn't satisfy me" "me neither now i know the diff. wouldn't it b wonderful if we were together right now and touching while we text?"

"that's wat I want. we're not like other couples. we were really together for short time so we know each other at a deep level"

"Im not happy with cyber relationship either"

"wasn't going 2 tell u, but u should know. have decided 2 try 2 sneak contact magnificus somehow. maybe they can use human assistant. intend 2 offer my services and ask 4 asylum. i think i have something 2 offer them"

"what about me? have u thought about me?"

"hope u understand, miss u but dangerous to go. will find a safe way for u to come later"

"i want to go with u"

"if we're caught they send us 2 hard labor camp 2 punish us. humiliate us, harsh real-life experience & no fantasy worlds"

"i know but i want 2 b with you even tho afraid if we get caught will never b together again"

"i have a plan. i have 2 work out details but might work"

"what u intend 2 do?"

"will tell my boss bot bout my new game I've been working on but say purpose is 2 sabotage magnificus. tell him magnificus might be interested and it will subvert them just like approved games keep population in line. will have to transport 2 magnificus 2 ship with game."

"u cant do that. ur game is 2 subversive here"

"have a sterilized version"

"magnificus won't accept u. cross contamination"

"have 2 figure out how to handle that. heard rumor bout possible joint AA-magnificus research/study lab. if true i go there."

"you've been planning this for a long time haven't u? y didnt u tell me bout it?"

"2 keep u out of trouble dear"

"wat happens 2 me?"

"i tell them I need u 4 my Computer Applications Director."

"what if they say no?"

"I'm good at my job. expect they cut me some slack"

Two weeks later they were working together at the Atlantic Alliance's new Study and Technology Center.

*   *   *

Even before magnificus started their proposed technology sharing with the Atlantic Alliance and its newly established Atlantic Alliance Study and Technology Center, it was obvious that to magnificus that their technology was well beyond Earth's capability to grasp. Earth scientists still clung to a version of quantum fields being the basis of mass-energy and therefore forces and particles, even though they knew the math was ad hoc and inconsistent, and the geometric background was emergent rather than fundamental. Magnificus must dictate some of the technological aspects of any agreement, but how to get the specialists on Earth to accept that? Would Carson have to send somebody down there despite the potential for kidnapping, capture of a shuttle with its devices and machinery being reverse engineered, blackmail, and contamination? The Center appeared to be staffed by robots and supercomputers, but three humans had been identified: Ben Richards and his two assistants, Megan Witherspoon and Peter Dolittle. It seemed that the latter mainly just wrote reports and papers that were copied to Renee Jaspar and sent to his superiors. Was he a spy or a saboteur for one of the other blocs? Carson and Newman debated what to do.

"I don't see any choice except to send somebody down there to straighten out the mess," Newman said. "Video meetings are getting us nowhere. Its taking way too long and Liu will find out the details of what we are doing very soon if he doesn't already know. If I was him, I would try to destroy our efforts with both the Alliance and South America by any means and at all costs. He has to try to close off every option except for giving him whatever he wants. If we send someone, we have to take every possible precaution and make it as quick of a trip as possible."

"It may be too much of a risk. A lot can go wrong."

"We have to work out the details to see if there's a secure way to do it."

"Good, please make a plan then, including all possible contingency scenarios and then we can calculate our best course of action."

"My plate is full. I would like to delegate the job to Renee Jaspar's assistant, Murray Hooper full time."

"OK. I want the full plan presented to me in 12 hours."

Late that evening, Newman, Carson, and Hooper decided what to do.

"First of all," Newman started, "We must support the Center and it's a big risk if we don't do something. We considered sending a robot to do the work for us, but we don't have one off-the shelf that could do the job and it would take too long to reprogram one, not to mention not having any spares or staff to do the reprogramming. I will let Hooper outline the plan."

"Easy items first. Whoever goes down there will wear an isolation suit with a 100% self-contained environmental control. The stay will be as brief as possible. Our representative will return first to the decontamination chamber and undergo that painful process while the shuttle returns under automatic control.

"Wright will be our point of focus and will have to give his OK before we start. We will dictate the agenda and send it to them just as the shuttle leaves. They will be expected to be ready and to proceed with the agenda the moment we arrive. For security reasons the notice we give them should be as last-minute as feasible.

"They will have to back up everything they are doing and send the backup to a safe place beforehand. There's a lot we aren't privy to, so we can only back up our correspondence with them.

"We will send only one representative who will be prepared ahead of time and have priority access to anyone back here who is called upon to assist.

"If anything goes wrong that cannot be immediately corrected, we vaporize the facility and everyone in it along with our shuttle. We will lose the facility, the shuttle, one of our people, and have to start over with our planning with the Alliance. We need to make that clear to Wright ahead of time.

"Someone could attack Annie's shuttle. We only have two of them. Recovering her shuttle is now a high priority while we are risking the other one.

"Wright will be advised that once the shuttle leaves, we will have to vaporize every threat at the first sign of trouble, so they will have an incentive to cooperate.

"The shuttle will be on self-surveillance at all times and programmed to neutralize any possible threat, valid or not. Shoot first and ask questions later.

"Our representative must be guarded at all times.

"We must insist that Wright establishes a no-fly zone for a 500-mile radius and tell him that we will shoot down anything airborne in that zone, but we can't notify him until 10 minutes before departure time for security reasons. We will also protect the shuttle on its way down and will respond to all potential threats to it, whether they be kinetic or radiation based.

"This is a golden opportunity for Liu. He just has to create a serious enough problem so we are forced to vaporize and do his dirty work for him. Have you considered that contingency?"

"We talked about it, but haven't agreed on the solution."

"Maybe there is a spy among them who won't hesitate to become a human sacrifice. And, how do we know if there are any robot spies programmed to self-immolate? Have you considered that?"

"We talked about that, too, but haven't agreed on the solution. Are there any humans on the inside who could be our eyes and ears?"

"One we know of, but we have no way to contact him and might jeopardize the whole plan if we did."

"Hooper, do you volunteer fly the shuttle and be responsible for this mission? If things go awry, we will have to vaporize you."

"I will go."

"Good, Hooper, please put all of the details in writing and bring it back to me in two hours. Then if the three of us agree on every aspect of the plan we will implement it immediately."

"When we are ready, I will inform Wright of our plans and let him know this is a test of his sincerity, and that we will hold him personally responsible if anything goes wrong, and if he is in any way culpable, we will react accordingly. I will explain that progress is at a standstill and we need this meeting to continue and insure a mutually beneficial outcome. I will also inform him that the face-to-face meeting is secret, and it will occur as soon as possible, as soon we can be ready, and it must therefore be at a time of our choosing. We will request that he start preparing for us right away."

* * *

Richards was busy working on his personal computer. The facility allowed him to use it off-network and off-line since he convinced them it was necessary for state security. But suddenly, a strange message appeared on his screen. He had been hacked. But how? The Atlantic Alliance must have a back door into his machine to keep tabs on him.

What choice did he have except to comply? He had black market devices he smuggled in including an old-style communicator. He tried to find a spot where the cameras and microphones wouldn't monitor him, a place he had noted already as he formulated his plans.

"Hello, Richards here. Who is this?"

"Call me Alpha. Not my real name. May I call you Beta?"

"Just call me Doctor. That's as non-specific as I can get. What is your position in the Atlantic Alliance?"

"I'm not from the Alliance and not connected with any bloc. I'll let you figure it out. We have to be discreet."

"What do you want? Be brief."

"We need someone on the inside. I will be meeting you in the near future, then it will be clear. Can we trust you? Do you know of any spies there you can name, human or otherwise? Any hidden agendas?

"I've been working on a new game. It won't be available to Earth people. The purpose is to subvert magnificus, turn them into game junkies, give them an erroneous and misleading impression of the Alliance. Would you like a copy? I can add some bells and whistles."

"Can you send it to magnificus privately, secure, and encrypted?"

"When it is ready. I will try to get permission from my boss to send it. He is aware it is an attempt to subvert magnificus. Otherwise, it will transmit slowly."

"Outstanding."

"I was given an assistant I didn't want named Dolittle. He's very smart and technically proficient, but no help to me. All he does is write and send reports. Draw your own conclusions."

"Let's cut this short for now. Goodbye."

How surreal thought Richards. Who was this really? Big red flag, better be careful. As a test, he would send coded information embedded in the game requiring a supercomputer to decipher. Risky, but it might pay off.

At 4:00 the next morning Richards was summoned to work. He was told to expect a visitor and not to ask who they were. He was also given a list of things to prepare and do ahead of time.

He immediately woke Megan and said, "We're summoned to work. Today could be the opportunity we talked about. Are you ready?"

"I'm scared," she replied.

"You can stay here. I've been careful to keep you safe. Besides, you know nothing about this."

"I want to be with you." She couldn't stop shaking.

Richards told himself he had to be the calm, alert, and careful one. He had to keep protecting her.

"Ready?"

She nodded yes.

"Keep quiet."

He used his black-market tool to painfully extract his and Megan's government issued subcutaneous GPS RFID tracking capsules.

"Ow!" She grimaced and tried to holler as quietly as she could.

"I know it hurts. Put it in your pocket. When we get to the building, I will plant them on a couple of robots."

Now the fat was in the fire.

* * *

Immediately upon Hooper's arrival a meeting was convened. Hooper had to remain in his suit and communicate through his translator, which however, didn't slow the proceedings down by much. They ran down the agenda item by item. Each party presented proposed wording when needed for commitment items and hashed out details until they all agreed on the terms. For the sticking points, technical items the less advanced humans couldn't understand, Hooper dictated the terms but included strictly constructed wiggle words and contingency actions to satisfy them. At one point Hooper interjected "By the way, thanks for the computer game. We don't have anything like it. Some of our staff are captivated by it and can't stop playing."

Richards recognized this coded reference right away, of course. As soon as he could manage it, he retreated and sent a private message to Hooper. It read "Dolittle foreign agent, his boss involved, I may become scapegoat, Witherspoon too, not safe for us here, take us with you."

The reply was, "need permission, my signal if ok, big problem for us." Hooper sent a coded message to Carson via the shuttle. Carson replied, "OK if Wright gives permission. Will make my best case we need them here. If yes, they could be an asset for us. All precautions. May not work out. Wait to hear."

Hooper immediately sent a coded message to Carson: "Spies in center, probably Liu's, Annie shuttle in danger."

Carson sprang into action immediately and called Holland and his defense center. "Holland, drop everything and find out who Annie might trust. Have them tell her Liu will attack her shuttle imminently. Tell her if she wants to survive, she has to return to the mother ship ASAP. We will protect her best we can." Next Carson called Wright and informed there were spies in the center including Dolittle and at least one robot. He asked Wright to secure the facility right away because he expected sabotage there.

Just as he was leaving Hooper gave the signal. Richards and Witherspoon rushed up behind him. Guard robots jumped in front to stop them. "Official business," Hooper said through his translator. "We have permission from Wright. Back off or all of us will be vaporized."

They backed away.

As they got into the shuttle Hooper motioned them "Stay here, strap in, snug up your head restraint, and don't move. Barf bag in front of you. Let me be upfront about what you have gotten yourselves into. We will all have to be de-contaminated including the shuttle, my suit, and your clothes. You won't like it. Then you will go to an isolation room and be tested to see if you harbor any bacteria, viruses, fungi, or parasites that might harm us. Some sample will be cultured and tissue tested. That may take 4 or 5 days and it will be more than just uncomfortable. If you are not cleared, we will arrange to return you to Earth somewhere, and someone will likely call you a criminal or a traitor and seek to execute you. If you are cleared, we may harbor our own organisms that are harmful or fatal to you. You take your chances. You will need to be monitored, and precautions will be necessary for many Earth months. On the way up we could be attacked and be destroyed or dosed with lethal radiation. Please prepare yourself."

Quite the bedside manner, Richards thought to himself.

As they ascended above most of the atmosphere, Hooper proceeded to deploy his shields and move radiation barriers over the windows.

Just then a flat voice droned from the control console "Six hypersonics from the North."

An instant later, lights flashed six times through the window covers and the shuttle yawed, pitched, and jumped violently. Richards and Witherspoon threw up. It wouldn't be the last time on this trip.

"Rough ride up?" It was Newman.

"Just another day at the amusement park." Hooper replied.

"We took out their missiles. From the north, so have to be Liu's. Targeting the launch sites and taking out all of his known spy satellites. All according to plan so far."

The success of particle beam weapons against most kinds of machinery was unpredictable. They would usually fry and degrade delicate electronic circuitry but the extent of the effect depended on whether the circuits were hardened. Components of lightly built parts such as airframes and stressed load-bearing frameworks could be weakened and destroyed, but heavy construction was more resistant.

They did not penetrate far below ground, although the atmospheric vacuum they created could explode shallow underground structures. Softer targets were the most vulnerable. Even if they didn't penetrate very far, the secondary radiation they generated could kill living things in underground bunkers. The degree of damage to the launch sites and other structures could not be assessed.

The shuttle accelerated quickly, and now leapt higher even faster that the hypersonics, but the occupants couldn't feel it much. It could also turn on a dime, even at Mach speeds, and thus evasive maneuvers were highly effective.

"We're almost there. Richards, Witherspoon, prepare yourselves."

For what? How could they be arriving so quickly?

"Incoming rockets," the flat voice stated.

"Must have launched them towards the mother ship in advance, anticipating your return. Diversion coming," Newman informed them.

By now Richards and Witherspoon were pale and petrified.

More explosions ensued, flashing white soundless light through the window covers. The shuttle bounced like a cork in a hurricane. The humans threw up whatever was left in their digestive tract.

Then there was a second or two, and then there was a final, even bigger explosion and buffeting. They couldn't see it from the shuttle but large pieces of debris were streaming away from the shuttle at high speed.

Hooper received a text: "Watch for the other shuttle. Protected it, same strategy. It could turn around and leave again, course unpredictable."

The fear was that Liu would realize Annie's shuttle survived, contact her, and she would be frightened into making a deal, maybe handing over the shuttle to him.

"We are maneuvering to hide behind the mother ship. That last explosion was one we set off and it propelled some debris, actually some dead Earth satellites we collected, away from the shuttle. We're sure Liu is watching with his telescopes, and we hope to fool him into thinking he blew us up. We are going to wait here until we're sure no additional attacks are forthcoming against the mother ship and it is safe to dock.

By now pale blue, Megan and Benjamin only marveled at the trip. "That was incredible," Benjamin said.

"We're safe," Megan replied. "Kiss me."

"First time above ground, first time kidnapped by aliens, incredible view of Earth, amazing technology we've only dreamed about, fantastic trip, what's a little decontamination after that?"

"Kiss me again before we find out."

* * *

"Liu screamed at Carson, "I know all about your secret meeting. Sorry I had to destroy two of your shuttles. I have spies inside your center who are sabotaging it as we speak. This is all your fault. You gave me no other choice. I forbid you to negotiate with anyone but me. You force me to draw a line and set an example. Next time I will destroy your ship and every one of you inside. You have nowhere to hide. You saw what I can do. Now give me what I want."

Nobody heard from Liu for the next 24 hours. Newman and Carson thought, he must be planning something and it was likely to be lethal. Does this mean Liu wants a war? What can we do to confuse Liu so he can't size up our capabilities? Time for Plan C.

* * *

Annie Koler presented a major headache and Carson didn't mince words. "Koler, you're a wanted criminal felon, you illegally stowed away, you stole a shuttle, compromised a weapon, destroyed alien property, consumed our precious resources, and you consorted with foreign alien agents without authorization. You have contributed nothing to this mission. These are all capital, treasonous offenses. It's my duty to discipline you, and I would be entirely within my guidelines to shanghai you on a deserted island in the middle of an ocean. Antarctica would be most suitable. Before I do that, I will give you an assignment and one single chance to redeem yourself. You will be watched closely, and if you commit a single further infraction, my judgment will be carried out. Do you understand me?"

Annie thought to herself, Carson was a pompous overinflated fur bag, she was entirely within her rights to take care of herself, who wouldn't seize their opportunities when they arose, and her opportunity to get even with them all would come sooner or later.

She held her tongue and simply said, "What do you want me to do?"

"We have already been attacked and that may continue. We have to defend ourselves without destroying any life or sacred property, if necessary. I want you to find and hack into Earth's military computers. Look for vulnerabilities and potential exploits. Find ways to plant malware and to disrupt these military computers that can't be traced, and make it look to them like malfunctions. Document everything but don't implement anything unless you receive explicit orders. Consider your job to be contingency planning. Remember that Earth's computers are more primitive than ours and the designs will be different. This is what you are good at and I expect you to be successful."

"What else?"

"Report to Newman. Follow his orders to the letter. Keep him informed of everything you are doing and why. Do not contact anyone on Earth and do not interfere with any computer without orders and permission. Is that perfectly clear?"

"Perfectly." She was about to add "Your Holiness" but caught herself at the last second. More strategic to be expressionless and hold her fire, she decided.

* * *

Thereafter, Wright assigned Taylor to be his chief point of contact with Carson.

Taylor's intent was to obtain the bulk of the contracts and subcontracts for the space elevator construction for the Atlantic Alliance. He also wanted expanded robot manufacturing along with improved automation and superior technology. He could promise tax breaks, unrigged competitive bidding with no kickbacks or bribes, subsidized transportation, and better logistics with the complex located in the Western hemisphere. He had the advantage that he was the only party other than magnificus willing to play the long game, even if it meant forfeiting his office. He was the rare politician willing to forgo short term gain if it meant his long term enrichment.

Taylor knew that the Atlantic Alliance had no suitable equatorial locations for a space elevator, so an alliance with LaFuentes was his best strategy.

Therefore, he figured on offering LaFuentes infrastructure expansion on her western coast, technical assistance with her own robotics and gaming plants, and the prospect of a backup space elevator on her east coast near the northern mouth of the Amazon to complement a west coast location.

To satisfy magnificus, Taylor assumed there would be a guarantee of equal access for all blocks and a multi-bloc security force to protect the facilities. The missing link was a way to mollify Liu, because unless he had major piece of the action and dictatorial control, he would try to sabotage the project.

Taylor figured that other Atlantic Alliance and South American Bloc politicians would naturally expect lucrative bribes, kickbacks, ownership stakes, and the like as the natural order of things. President Wright would be a particular problem in this regard. Neither Taylor nor magnificus was in a position to agree to corrupt practices.

The first "secret" negotiation between Taylor, LaFuentes, and their advisors was arranged. Carson would join them if a basic understanding could be worked out. Liu would then be brought in later; there was not likely to be any agreement otherwise. Taylor pitched his deal to LaFuentes and Carson via video phone from his office.

"Big deal," Edwina said on behalf of LaFuentes. "You offer me a few new highways, a new port, a few high-speed communication links, and some factory updates. It's a drop in the bucket. You'll have to offer me a lot more than that. I need infrastructure that reaches everyone in my territory and I want priority access to magnificus' particle beam weapon. Just how do you expect me to protect the facility without the weapon?"

"Everybody wants the weapon," Taylor responded. "It has to remain under magnificus control or else sooner or later one of the blocs will use it to start a global war and try to conquer the world. That's non-negotiable."

"How do we know magnificus won't use it to take over themselves?" Edwina returned. "Maybe magnificus has secret plans and they're stringing us along. Maybe magnificus thinks we're all stupid."

"Yes, we need some safeguards on their use of the weapon."

"For all we know, magnificus and the Alliance have a secret deal," Edwina alleged. "*I* want control or else no deal."

"I'm sorry but nobody will agree to that," Taylor replied. "We can find an agreement that benefits you and advances your agenda that includes safeguards on the weapon. We're offering you things you need so let's build on that. If we can't agree on a compromise Liu will insist on building in Indonesia. That won't help either one of us."

"So that snake Liu can get his hands on the elevator *and* the weapon?" Edwina retorted. "I don't think so."

"If magnificus has to go there, I think they will. Or the elevators can go in Africa."

"I can rule that out," Taylor interrupted. "Magnificus knows there's no long-term guaranteed security there, and the logistics are difficult.

"I think they will go wherever they have to, even if it's second best."

"We both know they will do whatever they think it takes to complete their mission," Taylor told Edwina. "It's the reason they're here. Let's agree on *something*."

"Alright but we can get a lot more out of those ugly little fur balls than they are offering. If I can't have the weapon then give me Panama and Nicaragua for a security buffer."

"They're not on the equator."

"That's my demand. Make me an offer."

"Let's be frank. The queen has family members who will rub you out and take over the first chance they get. That's your fate. Your hold on the population only reaches the major population areas. You need surveillance, computer power, high speed communications, spy satellites, and security. I'll talk to magnificus about how they can help you obtain all that and then get back to you later. We'll make sure you get everything you need as soon as possible. May I conference you in this afternoon at three your time?"

When everyone was ready, they held their three-way video conference with Taylor, Edwina, and Carson. A deal was worked out along the lines laid out by Taylor. The plan was to finalize the deal, present Liu with a fait accompli, and then attempt to negotiate with Liu and bring him in on it. Lastly, there would also be deals to include the smaller blocs as participating parties entitled to use the finished complex in exchange for helping to build and secure it. The key, however, was they couldn't predict how Liu would react.

"Magnificus agrees to help you to improve the volume, reliability, and sophistication of the robots from your factories starting right away, as you have proposed," Carson told Edwina. "We also accept both you and Taylor as administrative focal points, and that access to the facility by each bloc will be in accordance to their contributions to it. Since you are providing a location and local government that increases your contribution."

"Do you have a preference for the location?"

"We prefer La Mitad del Mundo for the complex because it has the advantage of higher elevation and a more defensible location. I believe Taylor has a plan to build out the infrastructure and defensive systems for the site subject to your approval."

"Is that acceptable?" Taylor asked Edwina.

"It's not enough," she replied. "Michael Mambler has asylum in my bloc and I want you to return his factories to him and allow him to export robots and telecommunications equipment to me. I demand you grant him a full pardon. I need his help to build out my infrastructure and to handle day-to-day factory production. I will offer you a share of his profits if there are any."

"Mambler is a fugitive and a felon. He was convicted of bribery and corruption and his factories were forfeited to the Atlantic Alliance government. I will be happy to negotiate favored customer export rights with special price discounts but the factories remain property of the Atlantic Alliance. I can't condone corruption and it would encourage other participants to demand bribes. We have to stamp out corruption, especially if it inflates the costs, stretches the schedule, or lowers the quality. Maybe we can grant Mambler a stay in exchange for cooperation. I will also agree to export robots to you at cost for five years."

"We agree to help modernize Mambler's factories in Brazil as much as I disagree with it. I'm not happy about setting an example by helping out a fugitive, but that's not my call."

"When are you going to drop this masquerade as an honest politician with real moral scruples? We both know there's no such thing and you're a sham. I'm getting really fed up with you," Edwina confronted Taylor.

"I'm interested in our common good, so I will interpret that as a complement," Taylor replied.

"I'm not finished yet," Edwina stated. "Swift promised me a free hand in Panama and Nicaragua. You've been jailing my operatives there."

"I doubt Swift agreed to anything, or if he did he wouldn't have followed through. Even if he did, I happen to know LaFuentes slept with him on more than one occasion. I'm sure he didn't want his wife to know about it."

"That's a vicious rumor and a lie. Besides, everybody knows mistresses are a perk of office. Swift gave me an ironclad guarantee."

"Can we stick to the agenda, please," Carson interrupted.

"We will work out an agreement to release your operatives and make guideline for your activities in Panama and Nicaragua. Since they are part of the Atlantic Alliance, we can't give you a free hand there."

"They are culturally part of South America. That has to be protected."

"It's a separate issue. I don't want to mix it up with this one. We can work out an agreement later."

"I'm not satisfied with that," Edwina replied.

Later Carson took Taylor aside to say "There's so much space junk orbiting up here collisions with the elevator ribbons are inevitable. We'll eventually need some space vehicles with laser cannons to clear debris in threatening orbits. We'll also need repair and maintenance ships in orbit. We have to include that in the details."

"I understand but we have enough to deal with already," Taylor replied. "I think it's better to wait to address that when the time comes."

* * *

After two more days of intense negotiations, the agreement was barely in place when the fireworks began, but it wasn't a celebration of the treaty.

Again the mother ship was buffeted with multiple flashes of light and a shower of shrapnel.

It wasn't unexpected. Shields had quickly deployed and one of the weapons returned fire.

Carson received a call from an enraged Liu an instant later.

"Tell me Carson, how is it you think I don't know what you are up to behind my back?" he fumed. "What you just got was a warning shot. I know your weapon will run out of fuel and particles sooner or later, then what do you think will happen? By sneaking around and not accepting my most reasonable demands, you are declaring war. You are an alien invader."

"You told me nobody gives a rodent's hind parts about a space elevator, including you, so what difference does it make to you where we build it?"

"Don't play me for stupid. You know this isn't about your precious elevators and spare parts, it's about who rules this planet, which means me, and certainly not you. I can easily destroy anything you and your new buddies build. You can't build anywhere except where I say, capuche?"

"But some of us have committed to an agreement now. We invite you to join us."

"And what is your pathetic little understanding worth? Nothing is what. It will crumble. I am willing to compromise and grant you the rights to build a space elevator in Indonesia under my exclusive control and protection. Now it's your turn to compromise."

"You don't have a viable location and you know my position."

"Then you will never get what you need. Your supplies won't last forever. You may as well be under siege. I can destroy you now, or just wait until you are desperate and give in. My conditions or no space elevator, no refueling stop, and no maintenance station, understand?"

"Sorry, Mr. President, you are mistaken."

Chapter Six
Alternate Plans

Politics is like a big game, or to be accurate, many overlapping games at once.

Carlson called Taylor. "Liu won't play ball."

"You don't understand Earth politics. We all have our spies. If anyone can gain anything at all by divulging a secret or compromising someone else, they will. Count on it. I told you to assume there are no secrets and watch your back."

"What do you suggest?"

"Damage control. I'll talk to LaFuentes's advisor Edwina right away."

Meanwhile, LaFuentes wasn't about to be pre-empted by anyone. She seized the initiative and called Liu herself, pretending not to know that she knew that he knew that she knew that they knew about the new agreement.

"Darling," LaFuentes insisted, "Wright and Carson are plotting behind your back. You're lucky I'm watching out for your interests."

"Sure you are. Let me tell you what I want from you."

"Let's talk about it in person. There's a luxury suite waiting for the two of us in my palace. I can make it worth your while."

"You're so predictable. You always play the same dirty game. Why don't you come here? I'll see you in *my* palace, but I can provide my own entertainment, thank you. What makes you think you're the most attractive woman in the universe? You're far from it."

"You're the only one who believes *that*. Every head of state gives up their secrets to my charms."

"Like Wright or Taylor? There's no chance you'll ever seduce *them*, so cut the chatter. You won't seduce me, either, because I'll take what I want from you anyway."

"And what may I ask is that? You overestimate yourself."

"Control of the space elevator and control of their weapon."

"I'd hand both of them to you right now on a platinum platter, but I just don't happen to have either one handy at the moment. You're in luck, though. I'm in a position to help you get them from magnificus at the present time, that is, if you treat me right."

"And just how is it you expect to be treated?"

"Magnificus are all a bunch of naïve morons. Now they're a gaggle of overgrown furry rats dutifully following their leader Lord Carlson around. Carlson thinks he's a furry supercomputer but he has to rely on Taylor. But Taylor is so irritating; he insists on his honest politician persona, but we all know better. I think his game is that he just wants some exalted place in the history books. I know how to use that against him. I'll put him in a position where he has to sacrifice magnificus for the sake of his sacred historic throne. You'll get what you want and then we ditch the lot of them, then poof, all gone, no more! So what's in it for me if I help you? I want Panama, Guatemala, and equal control of the weapon."

"Good luck. You can have territory but you can't have the weapon. What you get is my assurances you'll stay in power and anyone who opposes you will go the way of Taylor and magnificus, only instead of being flash fried, I'll give them just enough radiation for a fatal carcinoma, that way nobody will ever figure out what really happened to them."

"You're disgusting."

"But effective."

"I want equal control of the weapon so you don't rotisserie *me*."

"Look, I have operatives in touch with your cousins and your sister. Do you have a preferred method of assassination? Do what I want or else your reign will be a brief footnote in the history of the world. You'll just have to trust me to take care of you."

"That's exactly what I'm afraid of."

If it wasn't one thing it was another.

* * *

"LaFuentes ain't doin' me no favors," Mambler complained. "She's just impotent. All she can offer me is tax breaks, regulatory relief, and a small amount of capital. Totally lame. I'm lookin' for a better deal. You in, Wright?"

"Tell me, what did you have in mind?"

"My old factories and a pardon in exchange for a sizable percentage, all under the table of course. I happen to know nobody's gettin' anything while Taylor has the reigns. I know the payola has dried up and nobody around there likes it one bit. Maybe I can help you push him out. There's some developments here and an opportunity to do somethin'."

"I'm in charge of the Alliance and I can take of it all myself. I'll be able to help myself to whatever I want, so what the hell do I need with you? Besides, the government has already sunk a lot of cash into improvements to your factories and labs. Why should you be entitled to any of that?"

"Because with me you'll get what you want a lot sooner. How about a deal?"

"What's your angle?"

"I have inside information Taylor's trying to work a private deal with LaFuentes and magnificus to build a space elevator, but as far as those two are concerned Taylor's just a pimple on their nose. They don't want him involved. They really don't need him in my estimation. Won't do me much good either because no payola, so I don't want Taylor to have anything to do with it. They'll try to get Liu to join them but good luck with that. I see the situation as a chance to use Liu and LaFuentes to edge Taylor out and make the minimum of concessions to magnificus."

"Can you be a little more specific? What is your plan exactly?"

"I'm still working on that, and there are some other players we can use, but I think I know how to take control of it all."

"Call me when you have something more concrete. I'm busy."

"Tell me, Wright," Mambler pressed on, when are you going to set a trap for Taylor and get rid of him once and for all? He's a thorn in everyone's side. It feels to me like he is about to find himself in a scandal he didn't see coming. I don't feel like waiting and I don't imagine you do either. Our bank accounts aren't fattening the way they should be."

"What are you bitching about? Your margins and profits may have been cut, but you're still in business in South America. My bribes and kickbacks are dried up, so what the hell are you complaining about? I'm the one with the cash flow problem."

To be precise, Wright was also talking privately to Jack Ross, head of the Robot and Game Manufacturer's Association as well as president and majority owner of the Hypnophile Robot and Gaming Company.

"What are you complaining about now, Ross?" Wright asked.

"I don't like having to compete. It's not good for business. Destroys my margins. I'd rather pay someone off, namely you. We both gain even if you do squeeze my cash flow."

"Then you're no better off."

"Sure I am, especially if I get an exclusive export license for South America."

"And why do you think Machete Mike will tolerate that?"

"He's a wanted man and you don't have to give him a choice if you're running the show."

"I don't see any basis for a deal between the two of us."

"Don't try the hardball routine on me. Let's lay our cards on the table. We both know perfectly well that you have to depend on the robotics and gaming companies to supply the political class. If it wasn't for entrepreneurs like me, you would lose control of the population and the economy would fall apart. Robotics and gaming, and the companies that innovate and manufacture them, are the ultimate source of your money and power. Gaming companies create and produce the people's pacifiers. You need me as much as I need you."

To Ross everything was a game, a competition, including this negotiation, and Ross hated to lose.

"You're wrong about that. For every one of you who goes out of business two more hungry wannabes spring up to take his place. People like me are the ones who make the rules. We decide who gets the contracts, who gets to export and who doesn't, who gets rich and who goes to jail. The way I look at it, it's all about how many feathers I can pluck from the chicken, that's you, and still have him survive the winter and lay my eggs."

"Always so coy. The technology's too complicated for a politician to control it. Nobody else knows as much about as me. I'm not so easily replaced."

"Magnificus' elevators are the big chickens to be plucked now. If someone builds a space elevator complex, every company and politician will want in on the booty. Whoever treats me the best will get the reward. The way I see it, you'd better find a way to lay me some more eggs."

"Then suppose I help you depose Taylor? What do I get in return?"

"It wouldn't bother me a bit if somebody arranged for Taylor to be permanently indisposed. I might be grateful in a distant kind of way, but I can't be a party to anything like that. My hands have to appear clean. That sort of thing might happen unexpectedly, without my knowledge of it. Of course, I might happen to have a premonition of some kind, and it might happen to involve *you*, but haven't you heard of 'plausible deniability'?"

"You're saying you don't want my help?"

"No need for it. Taylor won't have his post forever, as powerful as he has become. There are ways to force him out. I have plans of my own and I don't need you at all. If you don't have a detailed offer ready for me, I have no reason to talk to you."

"Then wait for my details. We should talk again."

* * *

"Tell me, Edwina," LaFuentes asked, "why do we need the little people anyway if we have robots and computers to do everything? People are only good for certain jobs, and in the meantime, they have to be fed, clothed, housed, nursed, and pacified. What's the point of keeping them around?"

"My Shining Exemplar of Eminent Grace, according to a number of thinkers from more than a two centuries ago, dictators require their followers and the elite need their subjects. The will of the dictator can only be expressed as political power when the leader is widely recognized as charismatically gifted by the mass of the people. If the masses don't recognize his mission and his legitimacy, he will be perceived as an outsider and his power will not be accepted. The people are necessary to provide legitimacy, adulation, ego gratification, an ever-present verification of the leaders superior position and class, fear or other acknowledgement of ironclad power if that's part of the equation, and if it happens to be part of the governing rationale, recognition of the leader's spiritual and moral superiority. The leader needs those he is leading and the dictator needs those to whom he dictates to, but at the same time, the masses can be an expendable, superfluous nuisance all the same. If the leader is threatened like you are with your relatives, she may need the people's support to fend off threats."

"I don't buy that. Look, the people have to be watched all the time. All of them. The mob is fickle and they will throw us out if we give them a chance to think about it. They're all suspects and potential trouble makers except for the few who can prove to us otherwise. Especially the ones we blackmail and payoff, they can be the most troublesome of all. They have to be tracked, deterred, and rendered impotent. We have to keep entire complexes and buildings full of supercomputers occupied with tracking their every thought and movement, resources that we wouldn't have to bother with or maintain otherwise."

"Your Incredibly Enlightened and Superior Guiding Light, it's clear to me that predators are compelled to seek their prey, whether that's a food source, financial exploitation, power and dominance, or ego and status. A lot of the common people are surely expendable, but I think you need to keep more of them around than you realize or the economy will crumble along with your power. There aren't enough entrepreneurs, politicians, oligarchs, or elite classes to buy all the things the robots produce. There are no truly mass markets and there are insufficient economies of scale without enough people."

"The equation doesn't square on that one. The people don't have enough tokens to buy most of what the robots produce anyway, and nobody dares to tempt them to crave more than what we give them. That would be *really* dangerous. We had a consumer craze once and people everywhere got out of control."

"My dear Queen of the Thousand Continents," Edwina responded, "It looks to me like you have no good choices. What will you do?"

"You're my chief advisor. Shouldn't you be recommending to *me* what to do? One has to make her own opportunities now, isn't it?"

"But my Supreme and Masterful Ruler, if you deal with Taylor, Liu will plot your assassination, but if you ally yourself with Liu, he will get the elevator site and the particle beam weapon, and then he will get rid of you and take over your bloc anyway. You won't get technology or robots, and you'll either be somebody's puppet ruler or you'll be dead."

"So cheery. One must always deal from strength, or at least from treachery. We have to have the elevator complex and a technology upgrade. I *must* find a way to either get my own hands on their weapon or forge a mutual protection pact with magnificus to protect their complex and myself in the bargain. After that, nobody needs Taylor. He will just be a liability. I can offer him up to Liu and Liu can take over the Atlantic Alliance."

"My Omnipotent Lord and Master, Taylor is in bed with magnificus. Isn't that *your* normal position?"

"Watch it! Shouldn't you be working on a detailed plan?"

"Yes my Sovereign of Everything Above, Below, and Beyond, I will do so immediately."

The key might be that LaFuentes had the only viable locations while Liu was the most powerful and ruthless. They both wanted magnificus' technology and weapon. The Atlantic Alliance was dispensable. It looked to Edwina like a partnership was worth further pursuit.

* * *

Taylor was of course aware of his precarious position, and he was cognizant of the fact that the Atlantic Alliance had fewer bargaining chips than the other blocs. He needed to find a way to become essential to Liu or LaFuentes or both. His main asset was that he was in a position to sacrifice Wright and the Alliance, maybe oust Wright somehow and offer to divide up the Alliance's territories, or maybe to put the Alliance's substantial technological resources at the disposal of the others. He had no choice but to attempt his own secret deal if only to preserve his own skin. It would be a dangerous and possibly deadly game, but what choice did he have?

As a start, since the Alliance had seized Mambler's factories, upgraded them, and combined them with its own, then as Economic Minister he could offer first delivery on their products to LaFuentes. He could also corral the gaming industry into giving LaFuentes *its* highest priority and newest products. LaFuentes could grease the necessary palms while he kept his hands clean. Payments can always be disguised as shareholder dividends, study grants, management fees, and the like.

First, he had to talk only to Edwina and get her assurances their talks were strictly secret. Later, they could figure out how to bring Liu into the deal and what to offer him. As yet, although he had no clue how, he had the idea of somehow contacting Annie Koler about getting control of the weapon and offering her asylum and whatever else she wanted, that is, if Liu didn't beat him to it. Or, maybe he could work out an agreement that the blocs would jointly protect the elevators, only to have all of them except Liu pull their forces out so Liu could take over and withhold magnificus' use of the facilities in exchange for the weapon. The plan was vague and needed details before he could proceed, but it was, for him, urgent.

He told Liu, "Every other bloc is onboard with this agreement except you, so I'm offering my services. I'll talk to magnificus about our joint control of their weapon, but don't expect them to agree."

"Let *me* talk to magnificus about it," Liu ordered. "You have nothing to do with this anymore. The complex isn't even in your bloc. I want you to excuse yourself from this agreement entirely. There's no need for you to be involved. You're just an unnecessary middleman. I see no need for you to use the elevator, either."

* * *

Annie's secretarial-guard robot interrupted her as she relaxed her once svelte but now expanding, strapped-in body on her soft velveteen recliner.

"You have an encrypted audio call from somebody."

"Why are you tempting me, robot? Is this a test? I'm sure if its encrypted voice it's forbidden and I don't want anything to do with it. I know you are monitoring everything I say and do."

"Answer it," the robot insisted.

"Alright, hand over the phone."

Koler answered, "Whoever this is, I can't talk to you." There was a short series of intermittent clicks and the caller hung up. She knew from this code it was Liu. Perfect.

"Comb my fur," she commanded her robot.

Koler hacked the weapon codes once, so she was sure she could hack them again. Maybe she could hack into an Earth computer and send coded texts to Liu, disguising them as trial hacks. That might work. But while she was being watched continuously? And certainly, they are logging her every voice command and keystroke.

All the while, Annie's robot continued to comb her golden yellow fur.

She already knew Liu's sales pitch: "You don't need any of them and you have no future with magnificus. You can be free of them all. I can give you any life you want. All you have to do is give me codes and access."

And her reply would be the same: "Once you get the codes you'll just throw me aside like yesterday's garbage. How will you guarantee my security?"

But she had to solve this impasse to get herself a better life. And teach Carson and the rest of her oppressors a lesson.

* * *

It was of prime importance to Carson and magnificus to get the joint study and research centers rolling immediately. Carson first called Wright to agree on the necessary technology transfers, Earth factory upgrades, and equipment design. He also needed to agree with both Wright and Edwina on the security measures for when the time came to land the fabrication-construction factory ships at the elevator sites. This latter was a delicate matter since the Earthlings didn't know about the ships. For now, it would just be about "some of our equipment." At this time, he also had to talk to Edwina about LaFuentes's factory modernization and find out what official had been appointed by LaFuentes to head that effort.

Magnificus had to micromanage the work so it didn't result in non-functional, shoddy, unusable junk whose main purpose was a funnel to line the pockets of Wright, LaFuentes, Taylor, and the other officials and their cronies.

But, whenever Carson tried to reach Wright, he got a message saying he wasn't available, press 1 for this, 2 for that, blah, blah. So irritating. What was going on?

It was a similar story when Carson tried to contact Edwina. Not a good sign.

Carson called Zach Bender, head of surveillance. Bender was assisted by Megan Witherspoon. "Bender, is there any new intelligence to report? I can't get through to some of the Earth leaders. This is not their normal behavior pattern."

"I'll check and get back to you in twenty minutes," Bender said.

His report was, "There have been no news stories about Taylor and no messages we've intercepted since yesterday. We've seen nothing about state functions, meetings with legislators, or ceremonial or other events for the past two days."

That evening magnificus' orbiting systems intercepted a Chattertwit message from Taylor to the judiciary committee co-chairman: "Introducing emergency resolution tomorrow, Wright unable to perform duties, legislature directed to select replacement, prepare strategies for committee meeting. I expect to be nominated."

The agreement might now be in shambles.

"go 2 virtual park tomorrow. do u know anyone who has been there? nervous. dont know wat 2 expect," Joseph Chattertexted his gaming friend Tony from his apartment.

"nobody. only know rumors. few can go"

"wat rumor?"

"u have to be in top form. tough games, few win top prize, many r disgraced. how long u there?"

"1 wk. do u think anyone will know who I am? past champions? so embarrassing"

"nah, u won't know them, either, u only know their avatar"

ElectroWiz481 didn't have any information, either.

Joseph had to take a pill to sleep. He was too keyed up. A private robot limo car would pick him up the next afternoon at 1:00 pm and quietly whisk him a way to the whirring sound of its electric motor. It would be nearly a five-hour trip, traveling south, underground.

The car wound its way through a compact city past government and other sprawling buildings before entering the main highway, a crooked road through mostly deserted landscapes pockmarked by a couple of small towns. After a while it turned onto a mostly flat and wide multilane freeway busy with robo-truck traffic, still flowing past several other scattered small towns, warehouses, industrial buildings, fungus farms, and empty fields. Finally, it crossed a border onto another restricted freeway.

This was easily the farthest Joseph had ever ventured from home, in fact, he had never walked more than a quarter mile or so away, yet it was strikingly familiar. The sights and sounds were very much like many a trip in virtual worlds Joseph had played in.

A vague feeling of boredom increased and solidified as the trip wore on. Eventually, the car turned off the restricted and nearly deserted highway and proceeded down two successive bumpy two-lane roads for fifteen minutes until it pulled into a parking lot.

The outside of the thirty-one-acre park was not at all impressive. There was an asphalt parking lot with around a hundred spaces for robot cars and buses. A fairly large three-story rectangular brick building flanked a double-doored entrance and housed the extensive computer facilities, robot hangars, administrative offices, and equipment bays. Beyond that were buildings housing still more equipment, workshops, repair bays, projectors, and theaters. The main park itself was hidden behind a high concrete wall, but numerous towers jutted up here and there, both along the wall and inside the park.

The most interesting building, just inside the entrance, was a 40 meter long two story structure, with a sloped roof and with some rooms projecting outward, so that the lines of the building were broken and anything but straight. That was the dormitory where Joseph would be staying. A similar but smaller building nearby turned out to house guests and VIPs. Surprisingly, robots had to be content to closet themselves in glorified storage lockers when they weren't needed.

Joseph's car parked itself near the main entrance. A robot led him through the door, through a lobby, out a back door, and to the dormitory. Sensors detected him as he walked through and sent their input to a computer that automatically registered him.

His immaculate, second floor apartment felt quite luxurious. It was half again larger than his own apartment. There was a cathedral ceiling and the bedroom was a loft overlooking the living room, containing a modest half-bath and accessible by an electric lift. The kitchen was a bit larger than Joseph's while the bathroom on the main floor was adequate. In contrast, there was only one small closet in the entire unit. Textured gold curtains nicely framed the living room window and its fake view of a small fenced garden. The furniture was comfortable, high quality faux leather. Joseph had never been in such a grand apartment before.

The kitchen had a standard 3D food printer and processor along with a membrane computer console for fabricating meals and snacks. The highlight of the entire apartment, however, was the holographic monitor that covered one entire wall of the living room. A large, posh, swivel captain's chair with gaming controls in each wide armrest stood in the middle of the room facing the monitor, accompanied by side trays for hand-held controls, food, and beverages. Bread and circuses were conveniently within fifteen feet of each other.

It was six thirty in the evening by now. Joseph was hungry and becoming a bit tired, so he keyed in an order for a sandwich and chips to eat, and grabbed a beer from the refrigerator. He eschewed the dinette table and chair and instead sank into the couch, food in hand.

Just as he was finishing his meal, the screen suddenly lit up. An avatar greeted him, an icy, masculine figure with a crown like flaming steel, a gold metal warrior's vest, and a red jeweled medallion on a multicolored ribbon around its neck. It was a most intimidating presence. "Welcome to your home for the next week. Get a good night's sleep and enjoy tomorrow's game."

Joseph's orientation was scheduled for nine the next morning. The holographic screen lit up right on schedule.

"Welcome to International Virtual Theme Park," said the most resplendent avatar he had ever witnessed (but if anyone asked, he would have to say that President Liu's and President Wright's were better). "It is a rare privilege to be here and you are one of the fortunate few to be chosen. You are here because you are one of the top gamers on the entire globe.

"International Virtual Theme Park is sponsored by the governments of seven blocs. It is the most advanced park of its kind in the world. Only the best of the best are invited here. You are honored to be a guest.

"Games here are on a higher plane than any you've played before. You will play in the highest possible degree of virtual reality. Some of the games are played at a virtual reality console. You will play other games for real on the park grounds, in an authentic virtual reality.

"You will be assigned a different game every day, five total, each harder and more dangerous than the one before. The final game will last two days.

"The games here are not the politically correct versions approved for personal use by the government that you are used to. You must attempt to win by every possible means or you will fail. If you try to cheat you will be eliminated. You can enlist allies from among other gamers playing the same game at the same time.

"These games are deadly serious. You must win at least three of the five games you are assigned. You get two lives at International Virtual Park. Remember, three strikes and you're dead. You will not leave here alive if you fail.

"If you win all five games you become eligible for a special bonus game. If you win the bonus game, you will receive five thousand tokens and your choice of any apartment in any neighborhood those tokens will afford you.

"I will instruct you on the rules for your first game at one o'clock. Your game period will commence at one thirty and conclude at five thirty or when you are eliminated. Good luck."

Joseph was scared. This wasn't what he expected.

* * *

"Your first game is 'Hillbilly Feud'. Here are the rules. Commit them to memory before you begin to play this afternoon.

"The game is about family honor, justice, and revenge. It's about a family feud, but there can be two up to twenty-four families fighting with each other, depending on the number of game players. Some families can, and in fact will, form alliances with others for their mutual strategic benefit. These alliances can shift. You should look for alliances if there are more than three players.

"If you are good, you can expect to level up quickly during your four hours. At level zero, your family will have only five members, but you can recruit cousins from nearby states to come and join you. You can also entice members of other families to betray their kin and help you. Likewise, your own family members may be seduced into betraying *you*. Your goal is to eliminate at least one other rival family. You do that by either kidnapping, ambushing, or disabling its members, or by getting them thrown into jail. Jail is especially effective if the sheriff or judge is a member of *your* family, or if you bribe sheriffs and deputies or buy their election, because jailing a rival gets you twice as many points as ambushing them. Fists, handguns, and shotguns are the only allowed weapons in this game. No knives or explosives are permitted, but knives are a handy tool in this game and may be carried. You can lure your victims and plot ambushes in the farms, fields, barns, hills, outhouses, bars, saloons, barn dances, and other locales of the game.

"You get the most points for jailing members of other families and fewer points for offing them, but you also get points for stealing their hogs, horses, and cattle. You get points for selling your own moonshine, but a rival moonshiner might bust up your still so you have to retaliate. A revenuer could not only bust up your still but fine you and throw *you* in jail.

"You must always avenge insults, slights, killings, and arrests of your own family members, otherwise points will be deducted.

"Whenever you earn points, you also get an additional ten bonus points if you commit the act while barefooted. You can get bonus points if your act includes sabotaging a rival's outhouse or chicken coop, or wrecking their still. You can also get an extra fifteen points if you or any member of your family marries a close cousin.

"Getting caught with one of the ladies of the night loses fifteen points; not getting caught earns you twenty points. Likewise, if you get drunk and you are arrested for disorderly conduct, you lose fifteen points, but if you're drunk and avoid getting yourself arrested you gain twenty points. Getting into a drunken brawl results in the loss of twenty-five points and two teeth.

"The sheriff, if he isn't one of your relatives and hasn't been bribed, can form a posse and try to arrest you for stealing livestock or shooting or kidnapping a rival, especially if that rival was a member of the sheriff's own family. You could even be lynched or hanged, in which case you immediately lose the game, and so take care you are never caught. If you shoot an unarmed man or woman, you can also be hanged by the judge or by a lynch mob, in which case you will forfeit the game, so be sure they are at least carrying a knife in their pocket.

"Strict standards of hillbilly etiquette and decency are enforced at all times. You must say "May I?" and "Ma'am" whenever it is appropriate or you lose a point.

"You know that you win the game if you take out at least one other rival family entirely. You lose if they take out all of your relatives or if they take *you* out. Otherwise, whether you win or lose depends on whether you are in the upper one-third of the point totals. Do you understand these rules?"

"I think so."

"Good luck."

Joseph spent the rest of the morning going over those rules, thinking up strategies, and mentally rehearsing his moves.

Then, it was time to start the game. It would be played not in Joseph's living room, but out in the park itself with characters and scenery holographically projected. The projections were so realistic it was impossible to tell they weren't real.

Joseph was instructed, "You are 'Papa Joe-Bob,' patriarch of the Badger clan. You live in a double-wide on 4 acres. Your immediate family, all of them living with you, consists of a divorced thirty-two-year-old younger brother Billy-Bob, a fourteen year old daughter Emmy-Sue, a single good-for-nothing alcoholic twenty-two year old nephew-half-brother Larry-Bob, and a married twenty year old childless female cousin-niece Betty-Sue whose husband ran away, nobody knows where. Your main feud is with the Potter clan and their allies."

Joseph's avatar looked like a wrinkled sun-burned man with a long dark brown unkempt beard, a beat-up straw hat, denim overalls, a faded red and blue plaid shirt, and worn-out black leather farm boots with no socks. At least he was one of the few who did have shoes.

Papa Joe-Bob decided his first step must be to increase his family numbers. The more help he had, the more he could accomplish, and the better he could withstand any unwanted attrition. He phoned his out of state cousins to start arranging marriages. Larry-Bob and Billy-Bob were prime. He rang up ever-fattening third cousin Clara-Sue, a divorced potato chip queen with three children, a son Gerry-Bob aged fourteen, and daughters Peggy-Sue and Tammy-Sue, aged thirteen, and fifteen. Not only did he set her up to marry Billy-Bob, but as a bonus, all three of her children were also marrying age, and he could set them up, too. Very quickly Joe-Bob's family numbered twelve. He was still trying to hook up Larry-Bob with third cousin Martha-Sue, but she wasn't so sure she wanted to have anything to do with him, his rotten teeth, and foul breath.

Now he needed information about what other families were around, who his sworn enemies were, and who were the potential allies and enemies of his enemies. He grabbed his banjo and went straight to the poorly lit Mangy Dog Lounge with Larry-Bob and Billy-Bob for protection and cover. How could he tell which avatars were computer generated and which ones were real players he could team up with? He figured the real ones would either not be eating or drinking, or they would be pretending to eat the holographic fried possums and drink the computer-generated backyard mash. All of the men wore long-johns, dungarees or overalls, with plaid or flannel shirts. Most had some sort of hat. Some had chewing tobacco or smoked a corncob pipe. A few wore scruffy boots or old shoes with holes, though most were barefoot. Many of the older ones had moustaches or long food encrusted beards. He slowly moseyed over to a group of four at a corner table.

"Howdy, pardner. I'm Joe-Bob Badger. Don't recall seein' you around here before."

"Ain't seen you, neither."

"Buy you a drink?"

"Now yer talkin'. Name's Willy-Bob Temple. These here are my boys Clem-Bob, Timmy-Bob, and Billy-Bob."

"Pleased to meet y'all. Know any o' them Potter boys?"

"Why you wanna know?"

"Just askin'. Tryin' to stay away from that bunch, don't want no trouble."

"Matter o' fact, we're not too fond of 'em, either. That ol' man Bob-Bob Potter is one mean cuss. How big is yer clan?"

"Twelve an' growin'."

"Ya done rat well fer yerself. Thar's nine o' us here Temples."

"We's lookin' fer some hep. Ya got any clans lookin' to do ya in?"

"We're feudin' with the Cobbs and thems like hangin' with the Potters."

"Maybe if we hep each other we can all win this here game."

"That's what we're a goin' fer. Ah been talkin' ta the Russell clan but they'uns had some bad luck with their last alliance, lost a bunch o' family ta one o' them ambushes."

"Why don't I try ma luck?"

"Randy-Bob Russell is rat over yonder. Don't know if he'll talk ta ya, though."

Joe-Bob strolled past two tables next to Randy-Bob.

"Randy-Bob? I'm Joe-Bob, friend o' Willy-Bob. Can I buy y'all a drink?"

"Ah suppose so. State yer business."

"Ah was hopin' you'd reconsider an alliance. The three of us families."

"Ma last alliance was a bust. We had fifteen in our clan but we was hoodwinked and bushwhacked. Now we's down ta jus' ten. Might be better ta go it alone."

"A lot harder ta win, though. Who ya feudin' with?"

"The Dillons mostly, but they all got their friends an' enemies. How 'bouts you?"

"The Potters. Ah understand they'uns hang with the Cobbs."

"All three of 'em are friendly. They watch each other's backs."

"That makes it a might tougher ta win."

"Let me give ya some advice: These people may be uneducated and unsophisticated, but they's downright resourceful, clever, crafty, and self-reliant. Some of 'em have n'ar any morals along with the skills ta advance their dishonest wishes, some hang by their word. Don't you underestimate 'em. Some are just crude rubes actin' out their raw emotions with brute force, but then there's them are smart and knows what's a goin' on. Some are crooked as a stick, some's honest, hardworkin' folk. They ain't all one kind. Ya got ta distinguish which is what. Ma last partner underestimated some of 'em an' got all us'ns hornswoggled an' ambushed."

"Thanks, I won't forget. Did ya get yer revenge? Ya lose points if ya don't do nothin'."

"Tried ta get the sheriff ta form a posse an' go after 'em, but he was paid off. He just sat on his sorry butt."

"If thar's enough of us'ns we can elect our own sheriff."

"Yep. How many in yer clan?"

"Twelve."

"At least ah got a couple o' niece-cousins just tarned thirteen an' a boy sixteen now, all ready ta marry, so we'll be expandin' agin soon."

Thus, the Badger-Temple-Russell partnership was born. What should their next move be?

"Are ya knowin' how big that thar Potter clan is?" Joe-Bob asked.

"Mebbe fourteen, fifteen dunno fer sure," Randy-Bob replied.

"How 'bout them thar Cobbs an' Dillons?"

"Dillons I'd say are twelve or thirteen. Cobbs is a big bunch, I'd guess upwards o' twenty."

"We got us a uphull fight comin'. Our three clans can wipe out just one of 'em ta win. Dillons are smaller."

"An' smarter. They's the ones what wacked us. I'd go fer the Potters."

"We gotta protect ourselves from all of 'em," Willy-Bob added.

"We need good information ta work from. I got a idea."

The three of them snuck through the woods to vantage points they selected at the large Potter farm. Joseph was excited to be on his first raid. He like playing offense.

After a while, Willy-Bob saw ten or twelve of them come out their front door and pile into the front and back of two pickup trucks. He made his bird call, signaling Randy-Bob to meet up with him and Joe-Bob in the back woods. "Saw 'em a-comin' out o' the house an' take off in thar pickups. Cain't tell if anyone's still inside."

"I found the grandfather's still hidden back a ways. Time fer operation blackmail. I'll take ma ax and go there. Git yer shotguns an' cover me."

Just as Joe-Bob was standing over the still, ax in hand, a wobbly, barefoot, half-dressed spry old man in a green plaid shirt and blue jeans, with a long, tangled gray beard, came running up with a jug in his left hand and a shotgun of his own in his right. Joe-Bob jumped behind the still so the old man couldn't shoot him without messing it up.

"Git off ma property! Leave ma still alone, dang ya!" he shouted.

"We're gonna bust up this here still whether it's now or tomorrow or the next day," Joe-Bob answered.

"When the rest of 'em get back they'll blow ya full o' bullet holes."

Just then Willy-Bob rustled a tree so the old man would know there were more of them hiding in the woods.

"I don't care how many of ya there are, I ain't a'leavin'."

"Then let's make a deal. You tell us where your family is all the time and we won't keep bustin' up yer still ever day. Ya ain't gittin' no moonshine *ever* if ya don't go along."

"Alright, alright, Ah'll do what ya want. Jus' leave ma still alone."

"Deal, and don't tell anyone we was here."

The old man filled his jug, took a big swig, and started walking back towards the double-wide.

"Can we trust him?" Willy-Bob asked.

"Mebbe at the point of a shotgun," Randy-Bob answered. "We'll send somebody over here once in a while to give the old coot a reminder, like leavin' a smashed-up jug or a old rusty axe blade on his still."

It wasn't long before they found out where the Potters were going in their pickups. After they dropped off the eight riding in the truck beds at the Mangy Dog, the other four headed over to the Badger place. Billy-Bob and Larry-Bob heard them coming. They grabbed their shotguns and their women and headed for the woods behind their double-wide.

The Potters pulled their trucks up next to the hog pens. They grabbed four prime hogs, pushing two pair up a ramp into each pickup. As they got back in Billy-Bob and Larry-Bob started shooting at the trucks but to no avail. Both trucks hightailed it out of there.

When Joe-Bob got back he said, "Well Billy-Bob, they're yer hogs so what ya gonna do 'bout it?"

"Dunno."

"Yer a plumber an' a handyman, ain't ya? Ah'm a-tellin' ya what ta do."

Late that night Billy-Bob snuck over to the Potter place and crawled up under the double-wide. Inch-by-inch, as quietly as he could, he connected sink and shower drains to the water supply since there was a well but no toilet to pipe over to the faucets.

By then Billy-Bob smelled something awful from the crap in the drain traps. To soften the smell, he stopped to roll around in the pig wallow, then hurried home to wash and change, or at least switch to a cleaner avatar.

During the next several days, five of the Potters got sick, broke out all over, and went to the hospital for a good long time. They figured it had something to do with taking showers, and so every last one of them swore they would never shower again as long as they lived.

The day after Billy-Bob's triumph, the women were back at the Mangy Dog chugging beer. A well-dressed good-looking gentleman in a suit came up to their table and introduced himself. "I'm Professor Harry-Bob Dillon from the Greater Hillbilly University. I teach sociology and I'm doing some research. Would you beautiful young ladies be willing to answer some questions for me?"

"Sure," Martha-Sue gushed. "What ya wanna know?"

"Here is my survey," he said as he laid some papers down on the table.

They all watched him, and thus distracted six coarse looking men surrounded them.

"You will come with me now," the well-spoken professor told them. They made off with Betty-Sue, Emmy-Sue, Clara-Sue, and Martha-Sue, forcing them into the back of a pickup truck.

Fortunately, Peggy-Sue and Tammy-Sue were in the bathroom in their cut-off tops, short shorts, and high heels, powdering their noses and combing their long brown hair at the time.

Naturally, Joe-Bob was outraged at the kidnapping. His family was now down to nine.

"What's this here professor act? They's playin' dirty, violatin' the stereotype. That's outrageous cheatin'. The Dillons are in cahoots with them thar Potters and ah don't like it one bit. Ah demand a replay," he complained to Randy-Bob.

"Ah told ya ta be careful, they ain't all the same."

"Ah'm gonna get even with that professor varmint. Ah'll oil his clutch to make it slip, strand 'im somewhere ah can get my hands on him, and then ah'll fix the SOB real good."

"Don't be rash or they'll grab *you*. What else ya gonna do fer revenge?"

"Cain't arrange no huntin' accident. Too dangerous if they'uns have thar guns. Mebbe ah kin order me some piranha fish an' stock thar fishin' holes."

"Nah, that's too obvious. Ya have ta think o' somethin' else so it ain't clear to 'em what a-hoppened."

"Ah got ma own problems," Willy-Bob said. "That tramp Barbara-Sue Cobb with her boobs all a hangin' out plied Clem-Bob with some hooch an' challenged him ta drag race her brother-nephew. He had so much moonshine in 'im he crashed. Now Clem-Bob's in the hospital and ah done lost another fam'ly member."

Sometime after midnight, Willy-Bob, flashlight in hand, snuck over to the woods next to the Potter double-wide, dug up all the mushrooms he could find, and replaced them with poison mushrooms. Two Potters succumbed.

The next day, Joe-Bob found himself back at the Mangy Dog with his friends and relations. A well-dressed man approached their table. "I'm Clem-Bob Dillon. I teach chemistry at the high school. May I join you fine gentlemen?"

"Ah ain't a-fallin' fer this again," Joe-Bob said. "Ever body out."

"Let's clear outta here," Willy-Bob echoed.

The Badgers, Temples, and Russells all took off running.

A couple of game days later, Randy-Bob told the others, "Ah been a'schemin'. Ah made a deal with the Pickens clan and we'uns done got enough votes ta elect Billy-Bob Temple sheriff in today's election. Go git ever one ta the polls."

No sooner had the polls closed at six o'clock than Randy-Bob told the others, "Git yer fam'lies together, ever last one of 'em. We's formin' a posse to arrest them there Potters."

"What fer?" Billy-Bob asked.

"Stealin' the Badger's hogs."

"Where's the proof?"

"Since when do ya need any? Yer the sheriff ain't ya? Ya got Joe-Bob's word."

"Now?"

"Rat now before they figger out what we're a-up to. We gotta catch 'em with their britches down, when they ain't expectin' it."

"By seven o'clock the posse arrived at the Potter farm and arrested six of them and hauled them off to jail. That is, all except Old Man Bob-Bob, who managed to slip out the back door.

"Got all of 'em except the old man," Randy-Bob said to Joe-Bob.

"How we gonna catch 'im?"

"That damn Bob-Bob is a right slippery fella. Cain't manage ta catch the SOB no way."

"There's more of us than there is o' him."

"Not fer long. He'll be ringin' up ever cousin fer a thousand miles around ta come here, and they'll be a runnin' ta protect the family name. The fust thing they'll do is bust open the jail. We gotta find 'im and stop 'im rat cheer and now."

"Let's go to his farm and look fer some clues."

"Alright but he ain't gonna be there. Ah imagine he'll be a-hoofin' it over ta the Cobbs and Dillons ta get some hep. Ah don't a-reckon goin' ta his farm'll do us much good. The varmint can hunt, fish, and live most anywhere by hisself."

"He might remember somethin' he needs to go back fer to hep him live in the woods if he hasta. Ah wanna take a look see."

"Guess it cain't hurt nothin'."

The two of them hightailed it over to the Potter farm.

"Sure stinks around here," Joe-Bob said. "They ain't cleaned that there outhouse fer a might long time. There's enough gas 'round here ta heat yer trailer fer a year."

"Yer tellin' me?"

"Tonight's a new moon. Nobody cain't see nothin'. He could sneak back an' nobody'd ever spot 'im."

"Then no point hangin' 'round ourselves."

"Ah want ya to set this here box o' matches rat next to that thar outhouse door afore dark, OK?"

That same dark night, as Bob-Bob Potter returned to get a shotgun and felt his way to the outhouse to relieve himself, he lit one of the matches to light his way. Suddenly, kaboom! The smelly gas ignited and Bob-Bob and the outhouse blew themselves to kingdom come. Nobody laid eyes on either one ever again. And that's how Joseph and his two friends won the game.

* * *

"Today's game is 'Paradise Pirates' the avatar on the holographic screen intoned. Here are the rules:

"You are a pirate, captain of your own ship with your own small gang. Your home waters are the Hawaiian archipelago. At the beginning you need to establish a safe haven and find your own lair. You make points by boarding cargo ships and taking their cargo, which consists mainly of pineapples, coconuts, and mangos along with occasional assorted jewels and coins. A gross of fruit is worth ten points. Jewels are worth considerably more. Both merchant and pirate ships will occasionally arrive from South America and other ports, ripe for the boarding. You have to bury the jewels and coins some place where they can't be found, but at the same time you gain many points by discovering and capturing other pirate's treasure. Better yet, start your own central bank and have it print lots of fiat coconuts.

"If you board a ship, be careful not to harm its passengers or crew, otherwise you will lose a hundred points and your game will become much harder to play. If you claim the ship as your own, allow them to return to shore on your previous ship. You want your victims to feel confident they will not be harmed so they will surrender meekly. If they have to fight you, they will kill some of your crew and damage or possibly even sink your ship, so don't give them any reason to resist.

"You can gain treasure by plundering a town, but don't be too late and try to loot a place some other pirate has raided first. You can force a town to pay you protection money, but not if another pirate has gotten there first. Do your homework and try not to raid a town that's under another pirate's protection or you will have a damaging fight on your hands.

"Your crew may become mutinous or at least drunk on pineapple wine, and if you don't discipline them they may take over and force you to walk the plank, in which case you will drown and lose the game. They may also refuse to re-board your ship when ordered and remain ashore.

"You gain points by collecting wenches but watch out! If the wench is too saucy, she may turn the tables on you and betray you. And don't mess with some other pirate's wench or he will seek his revenge on you.

"Your weapons are daggers and swords, flintlock pistols, ships' cannons, and dynamite sticks you can throw at close range. You can also try heaving coconuts and pineapples but don't count on satisfactory results.

"All merchant ships are armed with cannon. The waters are also patrolled by a local navy. There are storms and tsunamis triggered by underwater earthquakes that can sink your ship, forcing you to lose all of your points and start over, so keep an eye on the seas and the sky and always know where your nearest safe harbor is. You can capture another, better pirate ship and take its cargo, forcing its captain to start over and making him your sworn enemy, or another captain can do the same to you. Try not to run aground, fall prey to shore-cannons, or succumb to navigation aids someone has intentionally moved to lure you into rocky waters.

"The better your ship, the higher your potential score. Pinnacle class ships are small with poor shorter-range cannons and small cargo holds, but they are very fast and maneuverable, and can be handled by a small crew. Sloops are a little larger and hold more cargo. They carry better cannons. Although they are somewhat slower than the

Pinnacle class, they are still fast and maneuverable. Many pirates prefer them. The Brig class vessels are built to be strong and to carry ample cargo. They can also carry bigger cannons than a sloop. Their speed is reasonable but not fast. Brigs are used by both merchants and pirates.

"Barques, Fluyts, and Merchantmen are large ships used by merchants. They carry lots of cargo and heavy longer-range cannons for defense, but they are slower than other ships. Galleons are also large with good broadside cannons, but they are also slow and not maneuverable.

"Combat Galleons are usually navy ships. They are strong, well and heavily armed, fast on a broad reach, but slower on other points of sail. Frigates are also mainly navy ships. They are nearly invincible but require a large crew, and they are difficult to handle. If you encounter one of these navy fighting ships, the best advice is to run. Your best chance to outrun them is upwind if your ship is better on that point of sail.

"You will start with a Pinnacle class vessel.

"Beware! All of your crew members will get drunk in town. One of them could develop a loose tongue and divulge your plans to a prostitute who reports it to another pirate she has an alliance with, then almost anything can happen to you. You can lose crew members who contract STDs, then you have to shanghai a new crew member from somewhere. Make sure you don't get a fatal disease yourself. If you capture a larger ship, you also have to find additional crew members somewhere to man it.

"Remember these rules. If you falter you will lose. Fast ships may seem like race cars to you, but cars can't go upward and there are other important differences, so don't get overconfident."

So it was that Joseph Witherspoon became Weird Beard the pirate, with his brown multi-directional beard, long folded down black boots, Jolly Roger hat, and long reddish-brown top coat. He did not yet sport a peg leg, a hook hand, or an eye patch. Those had to be earned.

He had to formulate a plan. If he wanted to make a large enough haul of booty and get the points he needed, he had to have a better ship.

He guided his little ship to a dock and he and his crew headed for the nearest waterfront watering hole. His second mate Simpson, with his much plainer pirate avatar with a bandana tied around his head and a short sword tucked in his belt, spotted a shapely and attractive avatar, or rather, wench, of around twenty. She wore a knee-length frilly red dress, a low-cut white blouse, short black boots, a wide black belt, and torn black stockings to go with her long curly dark brown hair. He wanted her at once.

"Hey, doll, how's about you and me findin' a cozy spot?"

"Get your hands off o' me you fat stinkin' pig. Who do ya think I am, one o' yer cheap tarts?"

"Now baby, don't play hard to get." He reached for her but she slapped him. The rest of the crew started laughing at him.

"Bitch, what did ya go and do that for? I'm gonna teach ya a lesson ya won't soon forget."

"Wait a minute, Simpson," Weird Beard said. "I wanna talk to this wench."

"You just get away from me. Ya ain't gettin' nothin' either," she said.

"I ain't askin' for nothin' as lovely as that would be. What makes ya so feisty anyway?"

"I ain't one o' yer common tarts, I ain't. Anyone gets close I'll whip 'em good."

"Ya got a boyfriend?"

"Just what business is that o' yours?"

"I wanna know if you're attached ta anyone, that's all."

"For yer information I ain't but that's no reason to grab hold o' me. I can take care o' meself, I can."

"I can see that. Ever done any piratin'?"

"I ain't but I'd be good fer it, I would. I takes what I want and I can handle meself."

"If you have no master why don't you join me crew? I can use ya."

"I'll bet ya can, but I ain't gonna be used like that, I'm not."

"No, you'll be a bona fide member of me crew and earn yer keep same as ever body else."

"Then I accept yer offer as long as ya make sure that slimy bunch of pigs ya call yer crew keeps their filthy hands off o' me."

"Ye have me word on it. What's your name?"

"Just call me Floozle."

It was time to get serious and rack up some points. Weird Beard challenged his small crew to get drunk, but not so drunk that they couldn't stay out of a fight and stumble their way back to their ship. They managed 200 points that evening.

"Ya call this coffin a ship?" Floozle asked. "I gots a mind ta walk, I have. What kind o' mess have ye gotten me into anyway?"

"We'll get a better ship and you're gonna help. Ya wanna earn the respect of the crew don't ye?"

"What ya want me to do? Mind ye, I ain't gonna do no tricks just on yer behalf."

"Don't worry. I have somethin' more suitable in mind fer ya."

Early the next evening, Weird Beard saw a well outfitted sloop tying up further along the waterfront. He drifted just offshore for a while and watched through his spy glass as its crew tied it up and headed for another bar.

"Tell me, Seaman Floozle, can ya hold yer liquor?"

"I can drinks any one of ya under the table and go back fer more."

"Good girl. I want ya to go into the bar and get those men what got off that sloop ta buy ya drinks. Get 'em good and drunk so they can't walk straight. Make sure they swallow at least twice as much as you do. I don't want 'em in any condition to come after us. Simpson and me will be right there ta protect ya. Can ya handle that?"

"Watch me. I don't need any o' yer help, either."

"The rest o' you nitwits, sneak onto that sloop. Do it quiet and careful like. They prob'ly left a mate ta keep watch. Sneak up behind 'im, tie him and gag him, and throw the rascal in the drink. Think ye can handle it? When yer done get the tub ready ta sail. Wallace, yer in charge."

"Yes, cap'n," First Mate Wallace replied.

As the three of them entered the dim candle-lit bar, Weird Beard pointed out to Floozle the sloop's crew at a long table, keeping to one side.

She walked towards them. "Who's gonna buy a round o' drinks? I'm thirsty."

And that's how Joseph got his sloop, a cargo hold full of pineapples and coconuts, and a hundred and fifty more points. They had to scuttle their Pinnacle class ship lest it be used in their pursuit. They called their new ship "Easy Pickins."

Now Weird Beard had to find a safe haven. The former crew of the sloop would be out for revenge.

He turned to his first mate. "Wallace, where can we go ta look fer a lair?"

"What kind o' place ya want?"

"A place that ain't occupied where we can hide the boat but still get out and escape real quick if we have ta. Trees or a small cove to protect us from the weather, or else a good cove nearby."

"Me thinks me knows a good place ta look, back side o' Maui."

Weird Beard thought they found an unlikely spot, where nobody would think to look for them.

The next day, they made their first score, a merchantman with a full cargo hold, burying the mere handful of jewels and coins from their haul halfway up behind a waterfall, a difficult place to get to.

They continued to hijack ships but played it safe, building up merchandise, treasure, and points at an unspectacular rate, but surviving the game nonetheless.

"Cap'n, ain't ya buyin' no peg leg?" Wallace asked. "Me thinks ya should buy yourself a parrot. A parrot hears ever body talkin' an' tells ya their secrets, if they'll betray ya."

"In due time, Wallace, in due time. I'll get me the parrot first."

Soon they were out sneaking around the coast, looking for lightly armed merchant ships to prey upon. The found a Fluyt going downwind and came up from behind. The crew put up no resistance. They took twelve crates of pineapples from the merchant's hold.

The merchant was released and went on its way. Easy Pickins ended on a dead run with the trade winds directly behind. Suddenly, a Pinnacle class boat darted out from nowhere, also on a run, closing fast from behind, firing ineffectively and short from its bow cannon. Then a second Pinnacle class ship appeared a few hundred yards on a beam reach on the starboard flank, closing and firing its own bow cannon.

"Must be a couple o' newbies," Weird Beard declared. "They're in cahoots, workin' together. Hoist full sail, full speed ahead. Turn to port, broad reach. All we can do is jibe between port and starboard broad reaches."

"They'll catch us anyway," Wallace warned. "We got a hold full o' dead weight ta slow us down."

"Jettison the cargo," Weird Beard ordered. "That's what they're after. Quick! Faster!"

With the cargo dumped in the sea, Easy Pickins was lighter and faster, and so was Weird Beard, thirty game points lighter to be exact. "Port tack!" he ordered.

As expected, the two small ships dropped sail, preparing to load and divide the crates between them.

"Now we turn the tables on the bastards!" Weird Beard yelled. "Fall off, starboard reach, load the cannons, pass 'em to port!"

Now the two smaller boats were sitting ducks. Both were damaged by Easy Pickins' longer-range cannons. They quickly hoisted sail and took off upwind. Easy Pickens reclaimed its cargo and thirty points.

The game day was done. They headed for the nearest bar before returning to their lair.

Back in the lair the next morning it was nothing but "Squawk. Squawk. Squawk"

"Shut up ya stupid bird or I'll wring yer foul little neck," Weird Beard threatened. "Can't hear meself think."

"Cap'n, cap'n!" an excited Simpson cried. "A merchant brig just passed by goin' downwind. Didn't spot us, no activity on the bridge. Let's get 'im."

All hands scrambled on deck, hoisted anchor, set sail, and took off as the brig disappeared past their small cove. It would be a sitting duck. They would go after it on a broad reach from behind, out of harm's way of the big cannons pointed out from either side of the big boat.

And then, as soon as they emerged from their lair, there was the brig turned sideways to the wind, waiting for them. It was a trap!

They were sitting ducks as the brig fired a series of broadsides right at them.

The parrot screeched, "Squawk, now we got 'em Floozle, now we got 'em, screech, where's their treasure, Floozle? Screech!"

"That bitch Floozle did us in, cap'n," Wallace exclaimed. "She must 'ave made a deal with some other pirate."

"Don't ya listen to yer parrot?" Simpson asked.

"We ain't been on speakin' terms. Shoulda talked nicer to the damn bird."

And so, Joseph lost his second game.

* * *

Joseph's next two games were "The Ultimate Demolition Derby," which he won, and "Your Life in the Food Chain," which he lost when he messed it up, allowing the animals he was hunting to acquire their own guns.

Joseph gave up dreaming of the grand prize a long time ago, after losing "Paradise Pirates." Now his life was at stake and it all came down to one game. He would prosper or perish depending on the outcome.

Chapter Eight
Clues

Zach Bender placed a priority call to Carson: "This is urgent news! We are receiving numerous reports that Wright is dead. They claim he died in his sleep last night. Taylor has nominated himself for President of the Atlantic Alliance and the legislature has scheduled a vote for noon their time."

Carson immediately placed a call to Taylor, but all he could reach was a machine with a message that stated "We are unable to answer due to an unusually high call volume. Please leave your name, number, and credit card information along with a brief message and we will get back to you as soon as possible in a week or two." No doubt Taylor was busy twisting arms, slipping cash under the table, and making deals.

"So it looks to me like Taylor is staging a coup."

"Yes but if coups don't progress quickly they usually fall apart. My guess is that Taylor has less than a week to grab control."

But the vote was inconclusive. Not only did Taylor not get the two-thirds he needed, but he didn't even get half, despite being the only candidate. A new vote was scheduled two days later to allow time for other candidates to declare themselves.

But a few minutes after the vote, Taylor surprised Carson with a video call. "LaFuentes, Liu, and I have an agreement worked out," he said. "We've all agreed that this is the only deal you will get, take it or leave it. It's non-negotiable."

"And what are the terms?" Carson asked.

"You and I will provide the infrastructure, robots, and supercomputers LaFuentes needs. She will have guaranteed sovereignty with fully updated and equipped military forces for protection of her and the new infrastructure. We will grant you two elevator complexes in Indonesia and South America. Technology development will be centered in the Atlantic Alliance and distributed to the other blocks from here, all coordinated and overseen by magnificus. The Alliance will also be responsible for cleaning up space junk with your assistance. The elevators, infrastructure, and other resources magnificus needs will be given highest priority by every bloc. For LaFuentes, Panama and Nicaragua will become neutral buffer zones, all imprisoned spies from these territories will be released unconditionally, Mambler will be granted a full pardon by the Alliance, and finally I will get the weapon codes. I need to finalize a new deal before the next vote, so please give me your answer within the hour. Check with the others if you wish."

"We will consider your offer and get back to you" Carson replied. He hastily called a video conference.

"You know there are side deals, especially between Taylor and Liu, and nobody is about to tell us what they are," Bender said.

"How can we know if this is really our final and only offer?" Carson asked.

"We don't. Try to negotiate anyway," Newton opined. "Taylor needs a deal to announce to the legislature before the next vote."

"But he also has to get changes past Liu and LaFuentes. That will take time, and if they agreed the offer was non-negotiable it won't happen. Or Liu could demand more concessions every chance he gets, trying to push the boundaries."

"It's worth a try. What other choices do we have under the current circumstances?"

"If indeed Liu, Fuentes, and Taylor all agree, it appears they have us cornered. Looks to me like all we can do is decide yes or no," Bender stated.

"May I say something?" It was Benjamin Richards, the only human present at the meeting.

"Go ahead."

"Let Taylor stew. He needs to show the legislature he is their best hope, so he's desperate to announce a deal with us. And what if you make a deal and Taylor isn't elected? You've boxed yourself in. Even worse, what if Wright recovers or is still alive?"

"Why do you say that? I'm sure they killed him twice over to make sure."

"Powerful politicians always have look-alike doubles and avatars who serve as decoys for would-be assassins. So who did they take out, Wright or a double? Wright didn't get where he is by being careless. Maybe he even set a trap for Taylor. We don't know for sure if he is dead or alive."

"You complicate our options, but thank you," replied Newman. "We have to take the possibility into account."

* * *

After further discussion, they decided to call Taylor's bluff. Carson contacted him. "Hello, Mr. Taylor. I believe you presented us with an ultimatum. On our part, we must be prudent, and we cannot be entrapped in Earthly political intrigue. Therefore, we will be able to agree with your proposal if and when you are elected President of the Atlantic Alliance but not before. We insist on two conditions. First, the agreement has to be enforceable, in other words, we have to have iron-clad guarantees you will carry out your end of the deal; second, magnificus always retains control of our weapon. These two conditions cannot be altered."

Meanwhile, John Bennigan had a predicament, as did many other legislators. As Vice-Chairman, his action tended to sway other legislators as well, so he was triply vulnerable. If he backed Taylor, but Taylor wasn't elected, whoever did become President would get rid of him one way or another. If he didn't back Taylor but Taylor still took over, his existence was in question. Already he had abstained on the first vote. Worse yet, if Wright somehow escaped or recovered from an assassination attempt and Bennigan backed anyone at all, he could kiss all future plans goodbye. On the other hand, as Vice-Chairman, Bennigan had his own independent sources.

"Hello, Bennigan, do you have any information for me today?" Carson answered on a secure voice channel.

"Is our communication is still strictly confidential?"

"Always."

"I have clues that something big is coming down after the next vote, but I don't know what. Have you heard anything from Taylor or Wright?"

"I thought Wright was dead."

"I can't confirm that, but I suspect he may not be. I'm in a difficult spot. I plan to abstain from voting for any candidate in two days. Others will follow my lead. If nobody gets elected President, I think I'll be alright, but if one of them does, he will get rid of me, very unpleasantly, I'm sure. You never know what kind of shenanigans go on around here. Will you protect me if things go wrong? I think I could help you."

"You know I can't promise. I'll do what I can. I would like you to let me know as soon as there are developments."

"If I can."

Two days later, immediately after the vote, a legion of storm trooper robots descended on the Legislative assembly, dragging off every candidate and every legislator who did not abstain. While this was happening, Wright suddenly pre-empted every broadcast channel including ongoing games. "Three days ago, Robert Taylor and his cronies thought they assassinated me, Wright said, "but it was only an avatar under my control. As you can see, I'm still here. Because of his treasonous actions, Taylor and all of his co-conspirators are in custody and will be disposed of."

Carson saw all of this. He was worried. Was this Wright the real one or an avatar? If it wasn't the real Wright, who controlled the avatar? Carson shuddered and thought, what if Liu is controlling a fake Wright and Taylor was a stooge? What if a lot of other things? Could an avatar have its own avatar? Would Bennigan know? He waited to hear from one of them, not wanting to interject himself into Earth politics by making the first move.

A few hours later, Wright, real or otherwise, called.

"Do you know about all of the developments in the Alliance these past few days?"

"I've seen the newscasts. I was worried we couldn't talk the past several days. I'm glad to see you are doing fine."

"Just have a bit of housekeeping to do, nothing more."

"Did you know that Taylor offered us a new agreement?"

"I have my informants. Don't expect to hear from Taylor again. I have someone named Bennigan from the legislature who has agreed to replace Taylor as Economic Minister. You will be dealing with him from now on."

"My pleasure."

"If you will excuse me, I have some important action items to address right now."

"Thank you, Mr. President."

Carlson still didn't know if this was the real Wright, but at least he was more comfortable talking to Bennigan.

* * *

This was a golden opportunity for Liu. The inevitable purge meant new people in power positions in the Alliance, people he could blackmail, bribe, and compromise. He called his head of foreign intelligence operations, Vlatka Maylin.

"Compile a list of every new high level political appointee in the Alliance. Use as many of our agents in there as you need. Find out their personalities, talents, weaknesses, arrest records, criminal associations, scandals, foreign contacts, affairs, and all the rest, the usual dirt. Make it your highest priority. Make sure I always have an updated list. I'm going to tell Hovmann to determine what we can use them all for, now or in the future."

Meanwhile, Bennigan asked Wright for a briefing on the talks with magnificus. But before that could be scheduled, he was interrupted by a call from Jack Ross.

"Hello, Mr. Bennigan. This is Jack Ross. I'm calling because I had a deal with Taylor, and since you took his place, I intend to continue that agreement."

"Which was?"

"Taylor was preparing to absorb my competitors and then grant me exclusive rights to all games in the Alliance. He was also about to grant me exclusive rights to export games to South America. He understood the value of games since they can control the public even more so than propaganda. In exchange, the two of us were planning to split the royalties and, let's call it, unreported monetary exchanges. I'm sure you will find these policies personally advantageous, shall we say."

"Mr. Ross, I'm new here and there is a lot on my plate right now. Can we discuss this some other time?" At least that particular excuse was not only justified but useful while he could still claim it.

"Very soon, I hope. I will be waiting."

No sooner had Ross hung up than Bennigan got a call from Michael Mambler.

"Hello, Mr. Bennigan. This is Michael Mambler."

"Where are you? You're under arrest. You're a convicted felon and you should be in jail."

"But on the contrary. Taylor had arranged a deal with magnificus. Part of it was that I would help out with the technology and in exchange, the Alliance would grant me a full pardon and restore my ownership of my old factories, including the government improvements."

"Mr. Mambler, I'm new here and there is a lot on my plate right now. Can we discuss this some other time?" Maybe Taylor wasn't really dead after all.

Later that day, Bennigan finally got his briefing from Wright. He immediately called Carlson on their secret line.

"Mr. Carlson, I'm already in deep with you, and if anyone finds out we are talking, they could accuse me of espionage and have me executed. Are we still on a confidential basis?"

"Always."

"Wright briefed me on your negotiations just now. You know, we were together in the legislature for a long time. I tested him by making allusions to past members, discussions, and deals only the two of us would know about. He didn't pick up on any of it. I'm convinced he's an imposter. That's a problem for both of us."

"Thank you. That confirms one of my suspicions."

"Do you know if someone else is controlling him?"

"Not right now."

Halfway around the world Maylin was briefing Liu.

"Wright has some assistant named Patsy who is filling his new vacancies and making policy approvals for him."

"That doesn't sound like Wright. He's a micro-manager. I'm thinking this Wright must be an imposter. I know of only one man in the Alliance who could pull off such an imposter and be convincing, and that would be Jack Ross. What do we have on him?"

"I'll find out and get right back to you."

An hour later, Maylin reported back. "We have nothing substantial except a detailed personality profile. But that means we know his weaknesses, and they are winning, ego, and money. He can be had. He wants to control all gaming at least in the Western hemisphere, so that's an angle we can use."

"Good. We have to control Ross and make him one of our assets. Then, we can tell magnificus we will compromise and concede control of their weapon to the president of the Alliance, namely Wright. Wright should get the codes. If we control Ross and Ross controls Wright, we get the weapon. Let's trap him."

Maybe they were underestimating Ross, forgetting that he knows how to play games better than anyone. After all, he invented most of the currently sanctioned games and he relished playing them himself.

* * *

LaFuentes knew she had to do something now, but what? Who was the kingpin in the Atlantic Alliance now? Will they be an ally or a

friend? And what about Liu? A political upheaval means changes, so
Liue will certainly make a move.

"Your Most Universal of Devine Majesties, I recommend you
see if you can form a defensive partnership with the Alliance. We're
both weakened and Liu will make his move, but there is strength in
numbers, two against one. Maybe we can set a trap for Liu."

"How?"

"I don't know your Exalted Greatness, but there must be a
way. The key players are Wright and Bennigan now. Bennigan had a
long career in the legislature and showed no ambition for further
advancement. Wright is still the kingpin."

"And what if that doesn't work?"

"Then we should also make a secret deal with Liu, your Royal
Paragon of Wisdom. Say we will work with him to help get the
weapon if he can guarantee our security."

"How can we make sure of that? His promises always have an
expiration date. And I need help to protect myself from my sister and
cousins. Until someone updates our technology, I can't track them all
the time. Upgrades to my systems are still a high priority."

"We'll find a way, my Queen of All Truth and Light. Maybe
we can figure out a way to play them off against each other and get
the upgrades in the bargain. I will contact Wright immediately."

"Get hold of Mambler first. He is key to the upgrades we
need."

"Yes My Adored Monarch and Master."

"Madame Queen," Mambler had joined the meeting. "I am
more than pleased to provide whatever you need. All I ask in return is
restoration of my business empire."

"You mean restoration of your kickbacks and graft?"

"A small matter of semantics, My Queen. I'll be frank with
you. I offered to help Wright and Taylor if they would restore my
factories and give me direct access to power, but they both just
laughed at me. Now I want the last laugh."

"But that was before the coup attempt," Edwina replied. "The situation has changed."

"You are both dismissed," LaFuentes commanded.

Edwina called Wright.

"You lack a site for the elevator complexes and we need better technology," Edwina told Wright. "You need peace in Central America while you reconstitute your government, and identify and eliminate your opposition. We can enforce peace in the disputed areas. We both know Liu wants to take advantage of this temporary turmoil at both of our expenses. Our other differences are minor. I'm sure we can help each other. I'm asking for an alliance with you for both of our good," Edwina stated.

She continued, "Your people are busy so we want to rely on Mambler. To that end, we request a temporary pardon and a role for him in managing his former businesses. Of course, he wants more, but we can decide on that when the time comes. The queen thinks our only option is to agree and start operations immediately, before some other bloc has a chance to sidetrack or sabotage us."

"I will ask Bennigan to look at this and then we'll talk some more," Wright responded.

"I have one more suggestion: perhaps we can talk to Liu and pretend we want to help him with whatever his plans are, that way maybe we can try to find out what he is up to and warn you about it."

"That will never work. He will play you."

Ross was licking his chops. What other schemes were in the works?

Ross didn't have to wait long to find out. LaFuentes's sister Rosa called Wright.

"President Wright, I'm sure my sister has contacted you. Whatever she offers you, I can give you the same with less commitment on your part."

"And what is it you are offering?"

"Equatorial sites for magnificus' elevator complexes and Central America, managed by you. I will also promote the Alliance's interests in South America."

"And what do you want in return?"

"You know what I want. This is the best deal you could wish for."

"I will ask Bennigan to consider your offer. We'll talk again when time permits."

* * *

Of course, Rosa wasn't satisfied with Wright's brush off. It was time to hedge her bets. Time for a side deal with Liu. But before she could contact him, he turned the tables and called her first.

"Is this Rosa?" a flat robot voice asked.

"Yes, who is this?"

"President Liu wishes to speak to you."

"I am fortunate he has an interest in me."

"Hello Rosa," Liu said. "I've been following you closely and I want to offer you a path to the presidency. It will, of course, have to involve the unfortunate demise of your sister."

"And what do you expect to get out of it?"

"Your pledge of allegiance, to me. Since I will be the one who brings you to power, I expect your unflinching loyalty and subordination."

"And if I agree, how do you plan to dispose of my sister and get me the presidency?"

"I will convince everyone that magnificus is plotting to use their weapon to take over the entire planet and your sister is in bed with them."

"That much will work. Who hasn't she been in bed with?"

"It's clear to everyone she wants magnificus to build their space elevators in the South American bloc. People must question, why is that? The answer is because she is helping them to take over the world so she can share in their power and fulfil her dreams of world domination."

"And then you and I ride to the rescue?"

"Naturally, and then your sister will have to be imprisoned or executed for her crime."

"When do you expect to put this plan of yours plan in motion?"

"First we have to set the stage, then I take care of some loose ends with magnificus and the Alliance. When the time is right, I will give a speech about how I have discovered their plot and show some ginned-up evidence. That message has to be reinforced, and it has to build momentum over a few days, then after that I will ride to the rescue."

"We have a deal. Tell me what you want me to do."

Mitchell, Liu's assistant and hatchet man, knew about the scheme. He asked Liu, "Did she buy it?"

"Hook, line, and sinker."

"Are you really going to install her as head of the bloc?"

"Yes," Liu said laughing, "but only temporarily. I'm sure she has plenty of skeletons in her own closet. I'll find a way to expose her as well, dispose of her, and rescue her block from her myself. That includes planting evidence that she was working hand-in-hand with her sister and magnificus all along."

"If you will permit me to ask, what is your plan now?"

"I have six plans, Plan A plus five more contingency plans. I won't fail. Plan A is to get control of Wright's avatar, trick magnificus into giving Wright the codes, and then get the codes from him. If that fails, Plan B is to trick Koler into hacking the codes again and giving them to us, then I first use the weapon to wipe out magnificus including Koler, before turning it on the other blocs. Plan C is to cut a deal with LaFuentes or Rosa and use them to obtain the codes and compromise the both of them. Plan D is to bombard magnificus' mother ship and either disable them until they plead for help or at least deplete their power, their shields, and their other resources. Plan E is to capture the Atlantic Alliance and South America so magnificus has no choice but to negotiate with me alone and accept my terms, and finally, Plan F, which is certain to work, is to wait them out until their power and food are gone and I can dictate the terms to them. So, you can see that, one way or another, I win.

* * *

Wright asked Bennigan to find out what Taylor's last proposal was and to see of Liu and Fuentes were still onboard. They were, so Wright told him to negotiate it with Carson.

Bennigan called Carson to reiterate Taylor's last offer, including infrastructure buildout, security, the space junk issue, the Central American concessions, and the rest of it. But this time he noted that weapon codes would be handed over to Wright, not to Liu. He concluded with "Everyone here is onboard for this proposal."

Newman was also present.

After reflecting for a moment, Carson replied, "I have to consult with my staff, but personally, I accept your proposal except for one change. The weapon codes do not get turned over until the projects are completed and we are refurbished and ready to leave for our next destination. Otherwise, you could easily turn our weapon on *us*, and end your obligations that way. I am also well aware that once you have the codes, you will have no incentive to move forward with the construction."

"Thank you. I will ask LaFuentes and Liu to concur."

But Liu didn't concur. He wanted the weapon codes given to Wright up front.

"Why did you agree to hand over a weapon?" Newman asked Carson. "You know full well that there is sure to be a fight over it, and it may well change hands. Sooner or later some politician will use it against his rivals and there will be a world war."

"I didn't say we would give them a working weapon, and I didn't say it wouldn't be depleted."

"What if they want a demonstration?"

"We have other weapons. If we have to sacrifice one we can."

* * *

"I'm really uncomfortable," Carson addressed some of his staff, "because we have very little insight about what kind of politics, what kinds of plotting and scheming, are going on down there that involve *us*."

"I have an idea but I don't know if it will work," Richards said. "Megan and I can pursue this one with your support. You know my job as a neurochemical engineer is to see to it that every game is designed to elicit the maximum possible emotional response from each and every gamer. How does anyone know that the politically correct response is really there? How do the computers know which games are the most addicting for each individual player?"

"I can't wait to hear this," Forbes said. "I want to know if anyone on this planet is messing with *my* mind or the minds of my fellow magnificus."

"I'll tell you one way they do it. Every button and key and joystick has built-in biometric sensors. Skin galvanic responses, pulse rates, subcutaneous arterial oxygen levels, sweat production, you name it, and it's all measured in real time. Fingerprints are scanned, too. Every holographic screen has a built-in camera. The cameras are used to monitor facial expressions, to see if players are concentrating and fully absorbed, if they are becoming bored or frustrated, and if they are feeling the emotions the games intend to produce as shown by their facial movements and body language. The data is all crunched and stored by banks of supercomputers. For every single gamer, the computers know if the games are eliciting the desired biochemical, emotional, and psychological responses. Because of my work, I had access to that data."

"How does that help?" Forbes asked.

"If you can find a way to help me hack into Earth's gaming supercomputers undetected, and if you have supercomputer capacity available for us to analyze data, Megan and I can look and try to find out if anybody is playing games that simulate a real war, power play, sabotage or an attack against us."

"It could take months to do that and sift through the data. It's worth looking into, but I'm not optimistic."

"If it works, great," Newman said. "But, none of Earth's leaders would be directly involved. Naturally they have their operatives, instigators, agitators, hit men and fall guys we have to find in the databases."

"Maybe we can come up with heuristics to narrow the search."

"We'll see," Newman concluded.

* * *

It seemed to Mambler that he was getting nowhere, so now he had a new plan.

Cyber warfare had been a fact of life for over a century. Many levels of defenses had been constructed over the years but there was no perfect barrier. Highly complex systems are always extremely likely to have undiscovered bugs and holes that can be exploited by any smart machine clever enough to find them. Like quantum physics, the results carried an irreducible level of statistical uncertainty. Now that AI computers did the programming and testing, systems were complex beyond human comprehension. Minor cyber skirmishes remained a fact of life. It was often impossible to find out where the well-disguised attacks came from. To make things worse, the indeterminacy meant a well-guarded back door had to be left in these complex systems so some person or machine could get in to stop unanticipated carnage from progressing and to then attempt repairs.

Back in the South American bloc, Mambler had AI machines and engineering employees working for him who were experts in these computer exploits. That put him in the catbird seat.

Mambler explained his plan to LaFuentes and Edwina.

"Madame Queen, you, Liu, Taylor, Wright, all of you flatter yourselves that you're in charge and you run the world, but you are mistaken. Robots build, create, mine, grow, transport, and maintain everything. Artificial Intelligence plans, designs, directs, monitors, analyzes, and choreographs every single thing that happens on this planet. You give an order and it goes to a computer, but you have no idea how it will be handled, how it will be carried out, or where the materials will come from. You don't understand how anything works, and it has all become so complicated and interconnected that nobody else does either. Only a handful of elites, pampered human geniuses have any notion.

"So tell me now, Madame President, if anyone schemes against you, how will they carry out their threats? Where are the watchful mechanical eyes that can protect you? Where are the robots that would put the poison in your food or blast you with a laser cannon, and who has the passwords and the biometrics to instruct them to do it?"

"I didn't ask you for a professorial lecture on computer engineering. What's your point, Mambler?"

"He, or she, who controls the machines controls the world."

"You're a closet megalomaniac, aren't you?"

"Just listen to me. There are back doors into every one of these robots, computers, and mechanical intelligences. They were deigned that way so they can be aborted if they go awry. Now who do you think organizes and oversees the computers and the engineers and master robots who design, create, and control all of these interconnected machines? Not you, not Liu, not any politician. It's people like me and Jack Ross. If we wanted to change the world, we know the right buttons to press."

"You're telling me that you can get me what I want by taking over the world's computers?"

"That's right. Power and security."

"And what do you expect in return?"

"For starters, I want total control of the world's computers. All of them. I also want priority access to you, Your Majesty, if we reach an understanding. You know the rest. I want my entire industrial empire back, and I want a big cut out of everything, not just the scraps I've been getting. And just to make sure, Taylor has to go, for good. I don't like him."

"I'll just wave my royal scepter, then."

"No, we will make a plan together and I will alter the world's key master AI computers' prime directives to carry it out."

"But you only have access to your own products. You can't change the computers in other blocs."

"Did you forget already? Everything is interconnected. There are always back doors. Every machine is corruptible. I have supercomputers and staff who can figure out how to do what I want."

"And if I don't go along with your plot, I suppose you will find some other politician who will?"

"Right again, but I have to beat Ross to the punch."

"Then let's start immediately before he gets the same idea. Work with Edwina and give me a plan by this afternoon."

Since Liu was the most powerful and dangerous, his computers had to be neutralized first. They had to be hacked and data had to be scrambled. Liu must be fed dis-information, and his games and the intelligence derived from them needed to be subtly altered. They wanted Liu chasing his own tail because of bad information.

But there was a fundamental problem that he, and no doubt Ross, was aware of: There is a tenet in biology that form follows function. In other words, certain behavior becomes habitual and then anatomy evolves to make that behavior more efficient. Humans and all other animals are governed by deep seated instincts, or as the Jungians would say, archetypes, that dictate this behavior. This could be rigid behavior such as you find in insects, or the more adaptable amorphous patterns of higher animals. Computer actions are similarly and necessarily determined by prime directives, rules, goals, or sets of predetermined outputs, basic schema, and actions. New knowledge and methodologies are learned during day-to-day problem solving, so entire systems are evolve and are built up from the basic instincts or directives. Not only that, but underlying directives may be, actually must be, derived ad hoc, arising to deal with separate or changing aspects of the environment. All of this leaves much scope for internal conflicts.

The result is that removing and adding to the basic directives of a machine could generate unintended consequences, new conflicts, require new training, or even destroy the machine. It is all a very delicate and unpredictable business.

No point in confusing LaFuentes with all of this, but there were no guarantees, Mambler figured. He could be putting his head in a noose.

Mambler continued. "To neutralize Augusto, Rosa, and your other rivals, I can create new 'authentic' computerized documents showing that Augusto poisoned Hugo with the aid of the coroner whom he bribed, then administered the same poison to the coroner to cover it up. That would open the door for Augusto's imprisonment and execution. That might intimidate Rosa and keep her under Your Highness' thumb."

* * *

Over the years, Liu had been the recipient of more than his share of bribes, kickbacks, and return favors. Not that it would ever surprise anyone. All of those participants were determined to get their fair share. Everyone tried to unearth the details about their rivals' dealings to protect their own security, sometimes successfully, other times not. Liu and his top assistants Mason and Mitchell all had information about each other they had stashed away.

Mitchell was successful in stealing Mason's biometrics and finding out where he kept his storage dot with his information. That evening was the opportune time to use them to get onto Mason's office computer. He transferred Mason's file, including the details he had found out about Liu, to cloud storage.

Liu quickly found out and he was livid. "Mason, why did you store your personal files with your lying accusations about me in the cloud? You know perfectly well that everybody hacks the cloud. Guard robots are outside. You're going to prison, for good, and I will personally see to it you have the most miserable possible life there. A security robot is waiting outside. It will take you away."

While everybody knew what went on behind the scenes, the important thing was to keep the details hidden. If the details became public, Liu would be compelled to take action and find a scapegoat for the sake of appearances.

Now Liu had another distraction and could be forced make his move on the other blocs before he was ready to.

* * *

Talks about when to transfer the Weapon went nowhere. No compromise could be reached. Liu decided to put Plan A aside for now and focus on Plan B.

Chapter Nine
Success or Failure

Taylor was not summarily executed after all. Imposter Wright had an equally lethal fate in store for him instead. This way, Wright could deny having blood on his hands.

On the day of his disappearance, Taylor was escorted to a basement garage by two fully armed security robots. There he was shoved into a black armored robotic car, which eased out onto a driveway with an escort of four more armored security cars, two each front and back. "Where are you taking me?" he asked in a trembling voice.

There was no reply.

"Take me to the legislature at once," Taylor commanded.

He heard the four security cars turn away. The windows of his car automatically darkened. He tried the doors and the windows. Everything was locked. Lots of scenarios flashed through Taylor's mind, none of them pleasant. Most of them ended at the bottom of a lake.

The trip ground on and on, for nearly seven hours non-stop, the limit of the batteries' range for the car. All that was on hand in the car's cooler were a couple of sandwiches and some bottled water, food that made him feel groggy.

Finally, the trip was mercifully over. A robot escorted a wobbly Taylor into the first floor of a two-story apartment building.

Taylor found himself alone in one of the cramped apartments. He couldn't tell where he was now. The only clue was a large holographic screen covering one wall. The fake view from the living room window was that of a brick wall beyond a patch of grass. He tried the door. It was locked from the outside. Did the computer behind the screen have the answers?

There was a small kitchen with a 3D food printer. The personal robot chef and the garden-fresh fruits or vegetables he was used to were nowhere in sight. The only thing in the small refrigerator was a pitcher of water.

Suddenly the screen lit up.

A very magisterial avatar appeared, an unsmiling well-cropped black-bearded face with an elaborate jeweled crown and purple robes with white fur trim. A cache of medals and medallions festooned the left breast area of its robe. "This is a virtual theme park," the avatar informed him. "You will play for your life. You must play five games in six days and win at least three times. If you lose, you will die. If you win you will go free. The games will be stacked against you. Do not expect to make it out of here alive. Few people in your position ever do. Your chances are slim. Most fail to make it past their third or fourth game. You will receive further instructions later."

The screen went dark.

How could he possibly succeed? Everyone else who came to this place was probably a highly experienced gamer, indeed for all practical purposes, a professional gamer based on their daily experience. The only gaming experience Taylor had was with learning and training games.

Now it was making sense to Taylor why he heard former president Swift and some of the legislators talk about awarding trips to virtual parks to people they didn't like. To add to his troubles, he wouldn't be sleeping much that night.

* * *

The next morning, the avatar returned to the big screen. "Your first game is 'The Game of Politics'. The object of the game is to gain control of every bloc on Earth, all ten of them in this game, either personally or through proxy rulers you control. All the while, you must maintain your grip on office. You will start out as dictator of Alpha Bloc. Many others want to assassinate you or send you to a labor camp and seize power for themselves. You must detect them and eliminate them first. You can amass armaments, spread propaganda, expand your spy organizations both foreign and domestic, plant false flag operations, carry out covert plots and secret assassinations, play dirty tricks, extend bribes, make backroom deals, come to tacit understandings, make false promises, double cross others and be double crossed, secretly supply and fund subversive organizations, and instigate covert foreign and domestic plots. You will deal with other politicians, foreign rulers, power brokers, lobbyists, special interests, and public relations specialists. You can accumulate lots of impressive-looking medals to try to awe your opponents, but they won't be worth any points."

There must be some mistake, Taylor thought. He should be a natural at this. Indeed, he was and he won this, his first game. However, he knew each subsequent game would be harder.

As expected, the next morning the avatar explained that day's game. "Today you will play 'Your Life in the Food Chain.' You will eat and you may well be eaten, in which case you lose. The game takes place in Africa, Southeast Asia, and an out-of-control correctional school somewhere in New Jersey. The scene will change unpredictably. Watering holes are especially dangerous but you will have to visit one at least once. You can buy a scene change if you have enough points, for example, you can add or remove trees from a forest or grassland. Instead of your normal plain looking avatar with its business suit and thoughtful pose, your avatar for this game will start out with a simple loin cloth and a bow and arrow. If you want an elephant gun, shoes, or clothing that protects you from insects, you'll have to earn points to buy them. You earn points by bagging wild game. The bigger the game, the more points you get. Every animal is a man eater. Some of them hunt in packs. From time to time, you will be forced to hunt or hide at night when predators are most active. One other thing: as the game progresses the animals can acquire their own guns. There is a legal disclaimer: This game has not been approved by the SPCA or the Humane Society. Continued use may be fatal. If you experience frequent numbness or pain, contact your pharmacist. Not responsible for incorrect use."

This was not Taylor's cup of tea. He was cornered by a ravenous turkey vulture and eaten whole. He lost the game. Now he was becoming even more worried. He tossed and turned and didn't sleep well that night.

The next morning, the avatar reappeared on the big screen and told him, "Today's game is a turf war. You are a drug lord with no followers. You must recruit your followers and fight to secure your territory within your city and expand it by pushing out other gang lords. Use graffiti to mark your territory. Martial arts, firebombs, and automatic weapons are not permitted. Knives, fists, semi-automatic hand guns, threats and intimidation, and thrown objects are all allowed. Watch out for snitches and infiltrators from other gangs who spy on you, especially molls. Cars, trucks, and motorcycles are available to you as long as you steal them, but watch out for bait cars. The police and riot squads are your enemies but they can be bribed. Neighborhood watch groups can get you caught. If you are caught, you can still operate from jail, but not very effectively. Various illegal activities are available to you to earn points depending on what the police are cracking down on or overlooking at the moment. You need to keep your eyes and ears open every second to see what is coming down."

This was a dirty, disgraceful game, but ideally suited to Taylor's background and experience as a politician. He won this game.

Even with almost no experience, Taylor proved better at gaming than his captors anticipated.

On the fourth morning the avatar on the big screen explained the day's game. "Today's game is about shark packs, not the kind *you* normally deal with but the kind that swim in the ocean. It is a shark feeding frenzy game. You will start as the lead shark in a small pack of your own. Sharks will eat anything, including other sharks. In addition, there are packs of killer whales roaming the seas that will corner and eat sharks, including you."

Taylor lost this game. One more loss and it was over. Now it was do or die, and it would come down to the final two-day game.

* * *

The wall screen lit up. An avatar instructed Taylor on the rules of his final game.

"Your final game is 'Reverse Mouthman'. It is also the most difficult game of all. I don't have to tell you what is at stake. If you win, you will earn five hundred bonus tokens from your play at International Virtual Park. But beware! If you fail, it will be your final failure. You will disappear and be scattered in the dust of history.

"You will be hunted by the all-consuming ravenous carnivorous mouth. If it eats you, it will be for real. Your remains will be deposited on the grounds of the park. You must kill Mouthman before it eats *you*. Hunt and be hunted, but Mouthman will multiply if you allow him to eat. Whenever it eats a cat or a dog, it produces one offspring. If it eats a human, it will also produce offspring, that is, eating a teenager allows it to produce two offspring, while all other humans result in three offspring. It can also reproduce once for every dozen frogs, lizards, rats, or mice it consumes. If it finds a higher mammal like a horse or a monkey and eats it, a Mouthman will produce two offspring.

"You will start out with a single shot laser rifle. If you gain thirty points you can upgrade to a laser submachine gun for killing more than one Mouthman at a time. Remote Mouthman sensors effective from five hundred yards cost sixty points; a surveillance camera placed in a fixed location also costs sixty points; the cost of moving the camera to another location is twenty points. Upgrades can be purchased for your avatar. You can buy tooth-resistant armor, but it will make you slow and not so mobile. For two hundred points you can purchase a change of scene. Motorcycles are available but they are pricey, three hundred fifty points. You earn fifteen points for every Mouthman you kill.

"Mouthmen will pursue you through cities, malls, countryside, and deserts in modern settings and in an old west setting, all in normally varying weather. The background will spontaneously change at unpredictable intervals.

"You can form alliances with other gamers you encounter who happen to be playing at the same time, but they may bring additional Mouthmen with them if they have more than you do. You can purchase a phone to talk to a gamer you encounter for ten points.

"As you gain proficiency you will automatically level up and the game will move faster.

"If you are still alive after two days and there are still Mouthmen, the game will be declared a draw."

Taylor had two hours before the game started. He told himself to think systematically, to find an effective strategy and an alternate, and then to follow it consistently. He realized he needed contingency plans, too.

Where could he hide? What means of escape were there? How could he ambush Mouthmen? Could he use bad weather for cover? If he was trapped, how could he turn the tables and kill a Mouthman? Could he disguise himself? Was there a way to find allies to coral and surround the Mouthmen? That would be ideal, to trap them and kill them en masse. How could a surveillance camera help? Which accessories should he purchase? His offense was to kill Mouthmen. How could he starve a Mouthman? His defense was to prevent it from eating and to avoid being caught or trapped.

He had never played such a game before, so he had to catalog every experience once he started. He realized that his life depended on clear-headed thinking and avoiding panic.

* * *

Taylor took a look at himself. There he was, with a face full of stubble, in red sneakers, white gym socks, a grey short-sleeve sweat shirt, and black running shorts. The shoes and socks would have to go. They were too bright and too easily noticed.

He found himself in a familiar-feeling small city, at a downtown intersection busy with robot-limos and robot-vans. Somehow, he sensed there was a park nearby, running north-south through the middle of the small city along a creek.

Where is the Mouthman he wondered? Was it hiding nearby ready to pounce and end his game right then and there? Should he try to draw it out and confront it, and end the game quickly one way or another? What would he do if he was a Mouthman? Reproduce! He must stop it at once! Mouthman was probably looking for victims to eat. Maybe it was in the park ready to gorge on the plentiful supply of hikers and joggers, or for an extra desert morsel, maybe it was looking to snag one of the few people walking their dogs. Someone trying to protect their dog would be a sitting duck, and so would their pet.

There was a zoo in the middle of the park with plenty of animals to gorge on. Food and bait for Mouthmen. He would have to go there, but of course the Mouthmen knew that, too. The zoo must have fences and guards. Should he go to the other parts of the park? But Taylor knew the park was several miles long and looking for Mouthman there would be a needle in a haystack.

Where else could Mouthmen go, he asked himself? Where was the easiest meal in town? The humane society! Easy pickings, and the offspring can snack and multiply there, too. Fifty-fifty that's where the Mouthman goes first.

Those were fair odds, so Taylor hopped on his bicycle, the only transportation he was allowed to have, and headed to the humane society as fast as he could. Would it be there? Could he stop it from eating?

He turned down a quarter mile long residential street lined with small old brick three-story apartment buildings. The humane society building was at the end, an old house with a large attached kennel on concrete slabs along with a parking lot, surrounded by sparse grass and an eight-foot chain link fence with an entrance gate.

Taylor looked around. There it was approaching the gate! It was a four-foot-wide gaping mouth with lots of sharp pointed teeth and a slurping tongue, surrounded by a pair of fat lips, with two bloodshot eyeballs on top and two short skinny legs underneath. He could hear its ever-growling stomach. He ran to the gate, slamming it shut just in time, then blasted the creature with his laser rifle. That was fifteen points minus five for the bicycle rental.

Was that it? Game over? Why was he still there?

There was a rattling noise. Another Mouthman was trying to climb the fence in back. The first one must have eaten something or someone and multiplied already. He had to pursue the other one. The gate opened and the dog catcher drove out, the Mouthman sprinting after the truck and Taylor running right behind both of them but losing ground, again slamming the gate shut behind him. Mouthman was salivating over the prospect of eating a dog catcher with a truckload of stray dogs and cats.

Taylor had to stop the dog catcher, then stop the Mouthman before it ate a dog or the dog catcher. But next thing he knew, the Mouthman gobbled up a dog that had escaped through the open gate and instantly split into two Mouthmen. Taylor dropped to one knee and took aim, first shooting one of the Mouthmen, and then shooting out the right rear tire of the dog catcher's truck. With Taylor coming, the other Mouthman disappeared behind an apartment building. Taylor looked carefully, heart pounding, gun in hand. No sign of it. Was it heading back to the animal shelter?

At least he had another fifteen points, enough now to trade his rifle for a laser submachine gun. What he really needed, though, was a Mouthman detector to find the creatures and to watch his back.

Taylor jumped into the truck with the dog catcher and the two of them raced back to the shelter, flat tire and all, intending to lock the place down and secure it. They were just in time. The escaped Mouthman had eaten a teenage volunteer and multiplied again. The three Mouthmen were converging in the shelter from different directions. He zapped them all with his submachine gun and waited expectantly for the game to end.

Instead, he missed one of them and there was a sudden change of scene. Taylor found himself in a Western frontier town. He stood in the middle of a dusty road full of horse and Mouthman droppings, wearing a red and white kerchief, chaps, a red and blue plaid shirt, chaps, boots, spurs, and an eight-and-a-half-gallon hat. The Mouthman sheriff stepped out of his office into the street. Was there a Mouthman deputy lurking somewhere he wondered? Across the way was a saloon where he glimpsed three Mouthmen through the swinging doors, lined up at the bar. Was that all of them? What could they eat in this town besides *him*? There were people in the saloon and there were lots of horses tied up along the street. Were those the easiest meals? What about the cattle ranches?

The sheriff stood in the middle of the dirty street daring Taylor to draw.

"I know better than to draw on an experienced gunslinger," Taylor thought. "I'll cheat." He ducked and rolled behind a watering trough, sweeping his submachine gun in an arc, killing Sheriff Mouthman. What do they do to someone who kills a sheriff in this town he wondered? Do they hang him or make him the new sheriff?

A man came bounding out of the bar, a Mouthman in pursuit. Taylor zapped the Mouthman. He was racking up points, eighty-five now.

Was that man real or an avatar? Taylor threw a stone at him. "Ow!" the man yelped as the stone bounced off. The man picked it up and threw it back. It bounced off Taylor, too. They must both of them be real.

"Who are you?" the man in the buckskin shirt and blue denims asked, toting his own laser submachine gun.

"Taylor Earp," Taylor replied. "How about you?"

"Joseph the Kid."

"How many Mouthmen you reckon are in these here parts?"

"Four right here. The sheriff had two deputies and there's the two more in the bar. There's a bunch more in them there hills, probably headed for a cattle ranch."

"Do you know which one?"

"Probably the Circle Z. It's the biggest ranch around here."

"Let's go. Care to be my pardner?"

"You bet. There's no way either one of us is goin' to win by ourselves. The Mouthmen reproduce too often."

"Maybe they will reach an equilibrium where there' no more food left," Taylor replied.

"Except for us."

"Which way?"

"Follow me, but first we have a couple of drunk Mouthmen in the bar and two deputies in the street to take care of."

Just then Mouthmen started streaming out of the bar through the swinging doors, nine of them. They didn't get very far.

"Looks like a couple of people in the bar just had their last drink."

"Yep. You know, your avatar face looks familiar. Do I know you?"

"Robert Taylor, from the Atlantic Alliance."

"Can't be. Quit pullin' my leg."

"I swear."

"Nah. Taylor is in the Grand Office Building surrounded by security robots."

"You mean the robots that kidnapped me and brought me here?"

"I don't believe a word you say."

"As you wish. Right now we have some business to take care of."

"As soon as I use some of these points for a Mouthman detector."

"Same here."

Suddenly, the scene changed again. They were both dressed in blue coveralls and being chased by seven or eight Mouthmen through a giant sewer pipe, probably under some city. There were three more Mouthmen two hundred yards in front of them. Their lives looked to be over.

"Follow me," Taylor said. "I'm using some of my points to change my avatar."

Taylor changed to a skinny snake and escaped through a crack in the pipe, emerging on a city sidewalk above. Joseph did the same.

"Slick trick," he said. "Snake's eye view of a high rise."

"This isn't working," Taylor replied. "We need some offense."

"I have a plan. I'm going to buy a scene change and lure them in to corner me. When they swarm around me, you kill them all off. My life will be in your hands."

"I can't let you do that."

"Here I go anyway. Don't worry about me. Just concentrate and watch your back. Work fast but aim carefully and make every shot count. Aim to kill and don't be haphazard. Shoot the closest ones first."

The scene changed in the blink of an eye, a human eye since Mouthmen never blinked. Joseph was standing next to a lone oak tree in a spacious, sparsely vegetated hollow flanked by bushy hills on three sides. They were both back to the avatars they had started the game with. Taylor was kneeling on the peak of the hill to the right, submachine gun in hand.

Sure enough, around two dozen Mouthmen came pouring into the opening between the hills, zeroing in on Joseph, drooling and making their snorting and digestive noises. Taylor concentrated on firing as fast and as straight as he could, but there was no way he could kill all of them before they ate his brave, newfound friend, a friend who was making the ultimate sacrifice for his sake. Taylor's heart was sinking.

Just then, Joseph used half of his remaining points to change his avatar to a poison ivy plant snaking its way up the tree.

The carnivorous Mouthmen were confused. They paused. Taylor finished them off.

It hardly seemed fair. Joseph risked his life, yet he was down to his last forty-five points while Taylor cleaned up.

"Watch out behind you!" Joseph shouted. Three more Mouthmen were coming up the hill from the front and two more from the back.

"You shoot some. Get yourself some points."

Taylor got the ones in front but the other two were three feet away, gaping mouths ready to spring shut on Taylor's head. Joseph got them just as they were pouncing.

Taylor had enough points to buy a Mouthman detector.

"Are there any more?" Joseph asked.

"Looks like another dozen headed this way. That should be all of them."

"They're like bacteria. They just keep on multiplying somehow. This is no good."

"Let's get them. I've had enough of this game. I'll be the bait this time."

"It won't work again. They're onto the vegetable trick now."

"What's the point of all this, anyway? All of this struggle and raw emotion and for what?"

"Life's a game. Don't fight it."

Taylor used most of his remaining points to buy a motorcycle and the two of them hopped on and sped down the road to ambush the creatures.

One of the Mouthmen ran up and regurgitated a cow onto the road in front of them just as Joseph, riding shotgun on the back of the motorcycle, zapped it. They hit the cow and went sprawling onto the road. Joseph's submachine gun went flying. They positioned themselves, ready for a fight. They wouldn't go down willingly.

There they were, back-to-back in the middle of the dirt highway with only one gun between them, completely surrounded by the remaining eleven Mouthmen.

Things were looking grim.

* * *

Back on the mother ship, Carson and his crew were still trying to figure out for certain if Wright was real or an imposter.

"What was it you wanted to say, Dr. Holland?" Carson asked.

"I can't be positive, but I think Wright is a fake and it has to be Ross who did it. He is the only one with the expertise we know about. And I didn't find evidence for anyone rehearsing an assassination or a kidnapping, but I found a game console with Taylor's fingerprints all over it. He lost a shark attack game yesterday, and right now it looks like he's playing a game called 'Reverse Mouthman'. That means he has to be at a virtual reality park."

"You mean he ran away to play computer games?"

"No, he's probably playing for his life. He could be eaten alive at any moment. Richards tells us he always suspected they send people they don't like to those parks to kill them off. Ross and Mambler are the only ones we know of with the capability to hack palace security and reschedule virtual park activities, so one of those two was probably the finger man."

"Where is this park?"

"I don't know and there isn't time to find that out. We have to guess, pick the most likely location and take our chances."

"Rumor is there's a park in the middle of New York, but that can't be the only place," Megan said.

But now, magnificus was about to be pre-empted by more urgent matters.

"Koler, you said you could hack the weapon codes again. When can I expect them?" It was Liu using their secret tap code.

"I'm working on it and I expect you to keep your end of the bargain. Before I can give them to you I also need to highjack a shuttle and get myself out of here before you decide to blow up the ship."

"Just how many shuttles do you have, anyway? I already blew up two of them."

"Last one." Annie didn't want to give anything away. She couldn't trust anybody now and needed her options.

"You'll have a chance to get away, I promise."

"How do I know?"

"We're partners, aren't we?"

Annie tried to work on her exploits a few minutes at a time, several times a day, making her activities look to the spying secretary-guard robot like her normal assigned duties hacking Earth computers.

Nobody seemed the wiser.

In two weeks, she was ready. It much was easier to hack the ship's computers she was so familiar with than to break into Earth's primitive machines.

It was time for the most dangerous part of her plan.

She snuck onboard her chosen shuttle, entered the password and security code, and powered it up. She dared do no more than that, lest she be discovered.

Immediately, before anyone got wise to what she was doing, she signaled Liu and transmitted the codes.

Liu wasted no time, either. He suddenly pre-empted Mugbook, Chattertwit, gaming screens, radio broadcasts, and televideo communications worldwide.

"Attention! Attention!" blared a mechanical voice.

Liu's speech started at once. "This is President Liu Hyun, supreme commander of the Sino-Asian bloc. I have seized control of magnificus' laser-particle beam weapon. Few of you are aware of magnificus. They are an invading alien species that has illegally seized tracts of land all over the world. They pose a grave threat to the continued peace, harmony, and idyllic satisfaction enjoyed by all of earth's human inhabitants. This mortal danger must be eradicated immediately to preserve the utopian world order civilization has so painfully arrived at.

"In a moment I will turn this terrible weapon back onto the invaders who brought it here. In exactly five minutes, they, and the thousands of embryos they brought with them to spread like a cancer throughout the world, will be exterminated in a flash. They will disappear in the instant nuclear holocaust they intended to inflict upon us, the rightful inhabitants of planet Earth.

"You are fortunate I have been on top of this situation from the beginning, and I am prepared to act heroically, strategically, and in a timely manner to save all of us from certain annihilation at the hands of these space borne alien madmen.

"In consequence, following the aliens' extermination at the hands of their own weapon which I now control, and which will demonstrate the enormous power of this weapon, the leaders of every bloc are commanded to pledge their allegiance and subordination to me, the new Supreme Leader of Planet Earth. In return, I pledge to continue to protect the Earth from all outside threats in the future, and to preserve the utopian status quo so arduously arrived at by our predecessors.

"We have determined that Acting President Wright of the Atlantic Alliance and Queen LaFuentes of the South American bloc, have been plotting with magnificus all along. Regrettably, I have no choice but to issue orders for their arrest and summary execution. Peoples of the earth are commanded to support my efforts and the pending transition.

"Your day to day lives will not change. You will notice no difference between yesterday, today, or your life in the future, other than the security of knowing that our planet is now safe from every external threat."

Everyone, including magnificus, was forced to listen to Liu's speech.

"Does Liu really control one of our weapons?" Forbes asked.

"He's not predisposed to idle threats," Dr. Holland answered. "If he doesn't control a weapon he'll look like a fool in another few minutes. If he does, we won't be around to know about it."

"How did Liu get the codes for the weapon?" Carson asked.

"Annie. She can still operate a console from her compartment. If she hacked the codes, Liu has his own AI computers to figure out the rest," Zach Bender answered.

"Then this is it. We're doomed. Our mission is lost. Forbes was right, we should have stooped to their level to survive," Carson said sadly. "What is that smirk on your face, Newman. Did you have something to do with this? Or is that you version of gallows humor?"

"Annie does indeed have the codes. To the ladies' restroom. I spoofed her. Expect to be flushed."

The weapon fizzled.

Liu was livid beyond words. Koler had betrayed him and made him a laughingstock all over the world! Plan B was shot. Liu became obsessed to make Koler pay. For now, it was on to Plan C.

* * *

The good thing was that Ross was in the catbird seat. The bad thing was that he was certain to become worldwide number one most wanted, and there were no bonus points in this game. He would disguise his activities, of course, but once the politicians suspected he was up to something, their agents would be watching his every move.

The great thing about having an extra avatar or two was that you could be in two places at once. The dangerous thing was that the left hand usually didn't know what the right hand was up to.

It occurred to Ross that his Wright imposter was about to become quite the philanderer. And it seems that Queen LaFuentes hadn't been feeling her best lately. Let Operation Evil Twin begin!

* * *

"Mitchell, get me LaFuentes!" Liu ordered. "And where is Maylin? I need some information."

"This is Edwina. The queen is indisposed and won't talk to anybody right now. I can speak on her behalf, same as always."

"I want LaFuentes!" Liu demanded.

"I'm sorry, Mr. Liu, I cannot even speak to her right now."

"We had an agreement."

"I'm fully aware of it. We can do without the Alliance. Divide and Conquer. Do you have a plan to compromise the Alliance?"

"Certainly."

"And what role do you have in mind for the South American bloc?"

"I will inform you of that after my intelligence briefing. I have to have your assurances that you are still onboard."

"You have my word."

"I will contact you again in an hour or two, but I want the queen herself on the call."

"Alright. Goodbye for now."

"Maylin, what are Wright, Bennigan, Ross, and the rest of that bunch up to right now? What do we have on them?"

"Mr. President, our agents report that, as we speak, Wright is having a secret meeting with LaFuentes in Nicaragua. They were seen leaving a private room together, looking a bit disheveled, I might add."

"The double-crossing bitch. She's trying to seduce Wright. It doesn't surprise me in the least. I'm through with that ho. Where is Rosa? She's been waiting for her chance to off the queen for years. Her time has come."

* * *

"My Shining All-Knowing Wise and Powerful Majesty, are you feeling better now?" Edwina asked.

"What are you talking about? I'm fine."

"But when I asked your secretarial robot to schedule an appointment with you this morning, it said you were indisposed."

"Something strange is going on around here. Did Mambler screw up the computers? Where is he?"

They conferenced him in.

"Mambler, what have you done to my computers?" the queen demanded.

"Nothing, your majesty, I assure you. I've been looking for exploits against Liu's computers or the Alliance's computers, but every time I find something, it has been patched by the time I tried to download a hack."

"You Holiest and Most Sacred Mother of the Universe, it looks as if we are not the only ones starting a new cyber warfare campaign," Edwina opined.

"It's Liu!" LaFuentes exclaimed. "He must be monitoring Mambler and counter attacking our efforts. What do you think he is up to?"

"I don't know for sure, Your Grandest of All Monarchs, but we better keep a close eye on Rosa and Augusto.

* * *

"How do you plan to eliminate LaFuentes?" Mitchell asked.

"It has to be an inside job, by a robot gone rogue. The means, whether its poison, laser rifle, or something else doesn't matter as long as its quick and final. Rosa is the key, but since the queen would never see her, we have to give her a means to hack a palace robot. Maylin, it's up to you and your operatives."

"I'm already working on it."

But the next day, Maylin had more news.

"It's happening again. Wright didn't return to North American. An agent spotted him in Panama, sleeping with Rosa."

"Is there anybody we can trust in South America? What about Augusto? Rosa and the queen are two peas in a pod."

"Augusto is ambitious but he's not that bright."

"Ross is the mastermind behind this. He has to be eliminated. It's obvious what he's up to and it's the same old thing: form a liaison with the South America bloc and shut me out."

* * *

Ross was licking his chops. Liu had already made a fool of himself with his weapon fiasco. All Ross needed now was a coup d'etat. It was time for Liu to make one more major miscalculation. He already fell for the fake LaFuentes and Rosa. And Ross thought he knew just the thing.

* * *

"What are you doing about Ross?" Liu demanded.

"There is a slight problem but I am on it. Ross has created a dozen facsimiles of himself all over the place. Agents are working on identifying the real one."

"Waste no time! Kill them all! Now! I don't care how many agents we have to sacrifice; Ross has to go."

Mr. President, there is another threat I have to tell you about. Our intelligence reveals magnificus has been talking to Bennigan about a resupply of thorium in exchange for defensive weapons technology."

"That's good news for a change. It means magnificus is running out of resources faster that I thought. I have them right where I want them now."

While his agents were getting rid of Ross, it was the perfect time to implement Plan D.

* * *

Ross laughed his head off. In fact, all dozen of them. Liu fell for his fake information hook, line, and sinker.

Chapter Eleven
Emergency

Joseph and Taylor were surrounded by eleven ravenous Mouthmen. There was no way out.

"Is there anything Mouthmen are afraid of?" Taylor asked. "We have enough points to change our avatars one more time."

"No, but I have an idea," Joseph replied.

"You're a better marksman than I am," Taylor told him. "I'll try to distract them while you shoot as many as you can. We may be doomed but I won't go down without a fight."

"Here we go," Joseph said. "First, change your avatar right now."

The two of them changed their avatars for the last time. Now they too looked like Mouthmen. It confused the real Mouthmen for a few moments, long enough for Joseph to take out eight more of the creatures before they caught on. There were still three noisy, slobbering, stinking monsters left, about to pounce.

The stomach noises intensified as a Mouthman started to engulf Taylor's head. Suddenly, the noises stopped along with Taylor's heart. "This is it," he thought. "This is how it all ends." Daylight replaced the clouds overhead. "This must be what the brain does when the lights are about to go off," he decided.

But no, it *was* daylight and they were above ground. There were no longer any Mouthmen. The two of them were just sitting there in a large, desolate field. They saw nobody else and no buildings or landmarks.

"I never thought death would be so silent," Taylor said to the Joseph he imagined to be next to him.

"It's not," Joseph replied. "The park just shut down."

"I know. I'm alive in heaven. Where's my harp? All of the computers have backups and the backups have backups. This isn't happening."

"Real or not, let's high tail it outta here before the computers come back up."

"Where do we go? I don't even know where we are."

"Just head east. We're bound to come to something. We can figure the rest out along the way."

"Judging by the sun, east is that way."

* * *

"General quarters! General quarters! Shields deployed." a robotic voice called out. A few minutes later there were a half a dozen flashes of light and magnificus' ship jumped suddenly in an evasive maneuver.

"Who is attacking us," Carson asked the robot.

"Two missiles from southeast Asia and two from one of Liu's satellites," was the monotone response. "Ground base missiles shot down by particle beam."

Carson turned to Newman. "Do you agree we should jump to a higher orbit to give ourselves more maneuvering room and more lead time?"

"I think Liu may be intentionally throwing space junk, flak, in our path and we have no choice but to keep changing our orbit. Our shields were only designed to stop micrometeoroids and cosmic rays. They won't last with what Liu is throwing our way."

"My view as well." Carson commanded a higher orbit. "We are conserving fuel and this won't help."

"More incoming," the annoying voice declared.

After four flashes of light a new wall of metal fragments loomed directly ahead. The ship jumped.

"Any suggestions?" Carson asked.

"Do we know where their transmissions to us come from?"

"According to our sensors, Liu's calls come from the hotspot island off the Southeast Asia coast, Wright's come from the island just off the North American west coast, and Edwina's come from the hotspot just north of Venezuela."

"Just as I suspected. Blast the island off southeast Asia."

"You think you can melt a volcano?"

"Trust me."

"Alright. Tell the computer to fire away, full power. Then call Liu."

A minute later, nobody answered the call. All they heard was the irreducible background static.

"What are you thinking, Newman?"

"Judging from the type of radiation we saw, the hotspots have to be enormous fusion power plants, and those power plants must supply enormous co-located supercomputing centers. We didn't sense any high power, high voltage transmission lines or the magnetism they would generate from the islands to the shore."

"So if we destroyed Liu's computers the attack has to stop. Is that what you think?"

"Precisely, but we have to be sure. I want to destroy the hotspot in the middle of the Pacific. It is an order of magnitude larger than all of the other hotspots, and it's probably the link that coordinates supercomputers from around the world."

"Do it, maximum power from the particle beam."

No sooner had they damaged the island then Earth blinked out.

"What the?" Carson exclaimed. Instead of the blue, brown, green, and white world they always saw before, the viewing screen showed a planetary wasteland. And their sensors now confirmed what they were watching.

"What happened? How can damaging an island destroy the entire Earth?" Carson exclaimed.

"I think the only way we will get to the bottom of this is to make a short, surreptitious trip down there with our instruments and cameras to see for ourselves. There's no other way to find out what is really going on."

"Agree. Let's not waste time."

Chapter Twelve
Happily Never After

Carson, Newman, Forbes, Lewis, and earthlings Richards and Witherspoon boarded the shuttle. They landed in a field in the middle of New York.

Two thin, frail, sad looking humans just stood there, desperately clinging to one another, looking into each other's eyes expectantly, each trying to read and understand what was inside the other.

The earthlings left the shuttle and went over to them. Megan introduced herself, "Hello, my name is Megan and this is my husband Benjamin. How are you?"

"We are Kevin and Rita," the man answered in a soft shaky voice. "We've been blissfully married more than 20 years."

"You seem like strangers."

"I know Rita's avatar so very well. I'm in love with her avatar."

"It's the same for me," Rita added.

"But have you met in person before?" Megan asked.

"Hardly anybody has, it's rare," Kevin replied. "But the avatars are real, it's the same thing."

"You mean this is the first actual human to human contact you've ever known?"

"I suppose," Kevin said. "But there's no difference. The cyber world is all we know. That's what's real. Everything else is artificial."

Rita added, "I held my baby for a minute once, right before the robots took him away, so this is not new to me."

Megan and Benjamin exchanged a knowing glance. This was all too familiar.

"Are there more of you?" Megan asked.

"I don't think there are lot of us left, but who can tell? There's no way to know. We're all scattered about underground," Rita responded.

"Yes, that's where we used to live, too."

"Can't you fix the machines? I want to go back," Kevin asked.

Megan was so sad she could cry. "We've been watching Earth from the sky, but this isn't what we saw before now. Now we're trying to find out what happened."

"What you saw before was all a virtual reality. Almost all of the people you've met are avatars. Avatars are the same as the real people they're based on, so there's really no difference. Only cosmetic changes. It's just that avatars are immortal as long as they're still useful. They incorporate the essence of long dead humans."

"So, you mean that President Wright, President Liu, Queen LaFuentes, Taylor, and the other leaders are avatars?" Benjamin asked.

"I haven't heard of the people you mention, but I'm sure they have to be avatars, and the original humans the avatars represent died many decades ago," Kevin responded.

* * *

Carson was sick. This is just like Gwydion Prime. "How are we going to fix this place and build our complexes?" he gasped. "Where will the resources, the materials, and the worker robots we need come from? How will there be enough time?"

Addendum One
Characters

<u>Augusto</u> is Queen LaFuentes' first cousin who has designs on the throne himself. However, he is not all that bright and needs help to achieve his ambitions. As a result, he tries to lean on and ingratiate himself with others and comply with their wishes and schemes, especially Rosa. This dependency gives him something of a sense of security and support, and also helps him feel less vulnerable. But, it's a false sense, and he is easily duped and used because of his dependency, and because of his need to imagine that certain others are his protectors. He is highly vulnerable to being fooled, and is thus a danger to himself, but not to other politicians.

<u>Zach Bender</u> is magnificus' chief intelligence and surveillance officer.

<u>John Bennigan</u>: The long time Vice Chairman of the Atlantic Alliance legislature, he subsequently replaced John Taylor, Jr. as Economics Minister at Wright's request. His long and close association with Wright in the legislature gave him an understanding of Wright's motives, modus operandi, and expectations. They are like two prickly porcupines with a mutual understanding. Bennigan is ambitious, but only up to a point, and he satisfies himself with his current position. He has a measure of security where he is due to the amount of time he has been vice chairman and the resulting acceptance of this status quo by other politicians. While a few legislators would like nothing more than to challenge Bennigan, oust him, and take over as vice chairman, trying to move up to the vice presidency or another higher position risks Bennigan's career and safety because of the potential plots of rivals. He knows the ins and outs of his current position, and he has enough insecurity and mistrust of other politicians not to risk climbing further.

<u>Norman Carson</u>: Carson is the classic stuffed shirt, but one with talent and vision. He is a big picture thinker but is not good with the details. Unfortunately, many an unanticipated adverse consequence are hidden in those very same details. To Carson's benefit, he recognizes that he must delegate detailed planning to those more suited to the job, and is willing to listen to any objections to his strategies they might uncover. His values are absolute and unyielding. Most important of all to his ego is the belief that that magnificus has attained the highest possible intelligence, and that this is what gives meaning to the universe. Thus, magnificus mission of spreading its progeny far and wide is the ultimate sacred goal. Carson does not recognize that all values arise from archetypal patterns as filtered and interpreted by culture, upbringing, and personal experience, and thus there are no absolutes, but rather ranges of non-destructive and meaningful values. He is not receptive to the possibility (and maybe even the necessity) that, as in quantum physics, anything that is not self-contradictory and doesn't reduce to a nullity or self-identity, can and does occur. Carson is firmly in command and everybody knows it, yet he is not a dictator, he delegates wisely, and he earns the respect and loyalty of his subordinates. He quickly discovers yes-men and realizes they are fakes he will not tolerate, but on the contrary, he expects the respect, loyalty, obedience, trust, dedication, hard work, recognition, and even admiration of his subordinates, and this is where much of his emotional reward lies. Overall, Carson is efficient, visionary, logical, focused, an excellent long-range planner, and he is quick to size up every situation. He a no-nonsense instinctive leader, but is not receptive to, and has little tolerance for, the nuances of personal relationships and emotional subtleties, and tends to be socially unaware except as it relates to the dynamics of his leadership.

Peter Dolittle: Dolittle's personal life is a mess. He primarily seeks to attain the maximum benefit for the minimum expenditure of work. Therefore, if the opportunity arises for theft, cheating, affairs, or any other easy gains, he will take it. Dolittle is naturally smart and technically savvy, but he doesn't care to exert the effort to use these abilities. As a result, he was blackmailed into becoming a spy. As a lazy and careless spy, his activities arouse suspicion. Those he is spying on may have an opportunity to feed him fake, misleading information. But who is he spying for?

Edwina is Queen LaFuentes' chief advisor, confidant, and executive assistant. She wants to be the power behind the throne. She is secretly contemptuous of the queen, but uses her to exercise power (and vice versa). She wants and solicits the queen's approval, but at the same time denigrates any that is shown to her. She feels safest operating in the shadows, behind the cover of carrying out the queen's wishes. She likes the prestige this association provides her with, and wants to impress others with her brilliance and capabilities. Edwina and the queen use each other, a mutually beneficial arrangement they are both subconsciously aware of.

John Forbes: Exobiologist Forbes is straight-forward, likable, and good natured with a self-deprecating sense of humor. People like to tease him. He goes along with it, but in the back of his mind it bothers him. He tends towards caution, skepticism, pessimism, and conservatism, but in a crisis, he will rise to the top. His cautious and skeptical professional viewpoint starts as glass-half-empty, but is likely to improve from there as more information becomes available. While he is slow to see the positives in a situation, he thinks and feels out every situation and will eventually come around. He has a curious, observant, scientific mind and he is very smart. While his immediate feelings always direct his thinking initially, he can also step back and be objective and think in logical sequences. He understands concrete things he can see and touch the best, and that's why he was attracted to the field of geology. He tends to be resourceful and clever. Psychologically, he is something of the joker. Forbes' personality perfectly suits his profession, which goes well beyond that of an ordinary geologist. His chosen profession is extraordinarily demanding. He has to infer exoplanets' geological history, climate as it developed since planetary formation, evolving atmospheric composition, possible catastrophic and extinction events, habitability and possibilities for life throughout planets' histories, especially for potentially habitable planets, all based on the characteristics of planets' stars single or multiple, planet size and density, orbital parameters, perturbations and orbital changes induced by other planets in the system, characteristics of the star systems' galactic neighborhood and the systems' orbit around the galactic center, possible recent close encounters with other stars, possible exposure to past novae and gamma ray bursts, spectral analysis, and other scant clues. Mission planning depended both on his analysis, and on the results of probes sent to other star systems.

Antonia LaFuentes is secretive, suspicious, and somewhat paranoid, but for good reason. She doubts the loyalty of even close confidants other than Edwina, with whom she has a well-choreographed relationship and a subconscious mutual understanding. LaFuentes is shrewd and cunning, but holds her cards close to the vest so nobody except Edwina, her front-woman, can figure out what she is up to. She holds, even nourishes, grudges and the anger that goes with them until some future development displaces them. Being in her own mind the all-powerful queen, she is contemptuous of all others, though she ineffectively tries to hide this. She is jealous of her perks and privileges and enjoys the outward symbols of her high position. She demands to be honored and given her due. Her fantasies of a future expansive empire serve to further inflate her ego, although they seem like a distant hope most of the time. She immediately begins sizing up everyone she encounters to discover their usefulness and attitude towards her, and to assess any potential danger they might embody. She is calculating, and ethical questions are foreign to her mind.

Edward Holland, psychologist, knew from an early age he was on his own. His parents weren't reliably present so he learned to take care of himself. Fortunately, his high intelligence and practical abilities provided him with the means and the opportunity to become self-reliant and think for himself. Holland is tasked with understanding the human motivations, inhibitions, liaisons, capabilities, limitations, blind spots, unconscious compulsions, and abilities and lack thereof, as well as strategies they might adopt, subconscious and especially manipulative or misleading games they favor, and so on of Earth's leaders. This is be no mean feat, and success is highly questionable. The potential for misunderstanding is enormous. Dr. Holland has to realize and take into account his own biases and cultural and personal blind spots. Self-awareness is crucial, and knowledge of the myriad human and magnificus cultures with their unquestioned assumptions, rules, and blind spots, is crucial. All minds have a deep and often inscrutable and unreachable unconscious having a multitude of ramifications. There is a strong tendency to project one's own mental state onto both others and onto alien minds, to assume one's own unquestioned values and motives are universal. This is rarely valid. Holland is aware of these obstacles. Magnificus' base attitude of looking down on humans and all other outsiders doesn't help, either, and will lead to miscalculation. Self-analysis is part of every magnificus psychologist's training, but knowing about personal issues and being able to change or even just make use of the information takes a great deal of effort. All in all, it is not even known if awareness of one's own psychology, let alone that of aliens, is achievable to any degree of precision. Any intelligent mind is necessarily a complex system with built-in traps and contradictions. Complex systems can arise from the behavior of only a handful of elements with a wide enough range of potential interactions. Take the 3-body gravitational interaction problem (or 3 bodies with a single mutual force acting between all of them) as a limited, crude example. This appears to be a very simple system, but predictions of future positions of the three bodies usually have to be made via approximations and/or simulation, and even then, are valid only for geologically short periods of time. So, in fact, even this limited example is unpredictable and can therefore be characterized as complex. Holland has his work cut out for him.

Murray Hooper is one of Newman's assistants.

Liu Hyun put his calculated and carefully honed step-by-step plan to become the iron-fisted president and absolute ruler of the Asian bloc into action purposefully and methodically. He sabotaged and cast aside his competitors one-by-one until he reached the top. Liu is controlling, manipulative, possessive, and highly opinionated, the latter of which is fully justified by his habit of always being right. He views life as a fight with victory going to the strongest, most ruthless, and most determined while the weak get what they deserve.

He demands blind, unflinching obedience and confirmation, which never seem to be demonstrative sufficiently to satisfy his boundless ego. He always wants more. This makes him unstable, and his desires and megalomania magnify themselves over time. He becomes ever more grandiose, demanding, judgmental, and paranoid. Whenever something fails to go his way, or even when the credit and praise he feels are his due are not forthcoming, he imagines slights and sabotage by those around him. His demands become more and more over the top, with the demonstrations of loyalty he insists on entailing the self-destruction of his subordinates as proof of their commitment. After a while he became the cause others should dedicate themselves to, that is, he came to believe his own self-glorifying spin.

Liu has little patience for diplomacy, though he will resort to it if he has to. To him it is always non-binding. He prefers the direct approach, the iron fist. Brute force, bullying, blackmail, and the like get him more immediate results and thus better serve his ambitions.

Liu can be somewhat charismatic in public when it suits his purposes, projecting a great self-confidence, appearing to have absolute mastery of every situation, sensing and seeming to promise, or at least hint at, giving people what they want. His ability to sell himself, and his clever and slick packaging of his personality and views, draws in ever more followers who never examine the inherent contradictions, but rather rationalize them and brush them aside. Thus, he is perceived as convincing, even though he breaks promises as a matter of course, and always has a rationalization for doing so.

Liu is most arrogant in private. His narcissism means that different rules apply to himself than to everyone else. He is a pure user of others, all of whom are inferior, unworthy, and deserving of what they get. He always blames other people when things go wrong, then persecutes them with a vengeance.

All of this makes him susceptible to rash decisions, which can then be reversed based on mood shifts, making him arbitrary, unpredictable, and scary, but also making him vulnerable.

Liu finally progressed to the brute force stage, where all dissent and disagreement must be ruthlessly crushed. No rights, feelings, or possessions are respected except his own. Either a breakdown, a war, or an iron-fisted police state must now follow. At this stage, he wants sole control of the particle beam weapon, seeing it as his key to world domination.

Renee Jaspar is magnificus' brilliant chief engineer. She can be systematic, organized, and detailed. She dedicates herself to her work, but it never seems to help her that much with her self-image. Under the surface she is incurably insecure, and constantly seeks approval, acceptance, reassurance, and recognition, especially from her husband Forbes and rom respected superiors.

Annie Koler: Kohler is an accomplished criminal computer hacker and weapons specialist. Some people live and learn from their experiences and mistakes. Narcissistic types, on the other hand, double down on their beliefs and behavior until they become caricatures of themselves. Annie is one of the later. She wants immediate gratification and is driven by whatever impulse pops up from her unconscious and possesses her mind at the moment. Her thoughts and values are determined by her wants, and she tends to be obsessive about them. She looks for ways to extract the maximum reward from each situation with minimum risk. She has a number of favored means to get what she wants. Her first choice is by manipulation, bullying, intimidation, and invective. Guilt is her ally. This provides an ample excuse to pour out endless streams of venom on those who richly deserve it, at least in her self-centered opinion. If this tactic fails, she will try to seduce or manipulate with gossip. Annie views herself as a dispenser of truth, logic, and common sense. She knows better than everyone else. If there is something she doesn't know it is because it is trivial or stupid and not worth bothering about. The best way with people is to be up front and confront them with the truth of their inadequacies. Annie stole the codes to magnificus' laser-particle beam weapons and planned to use her control of them to dominate her fellow magnificus and any of earth's inhabitants who happened to annoy or irritate her. Her behavior proved to sometimes be unexpectedly burdensome to herself as well as others. Now she is trapped by her past and has to make the best of it. She has no choice but to continue the way she is.

Marie Lewis is magnificus' chief diplomat and negotiator.

Michael Mambler: Mambler wants to climb over everyone else to achieve the omniscient industrial empire that would validate himself and prove that he is worthy. He doesn't hesitate to resort to graft, bribery, sabotage, or any other means to achieve this end that he aspires to. He considers it his due to be filthy rich by any means. He resents and despises anyone who objects to his dishonesty or otherwise stands in his way. LaFuentes, Ross, and Taylor are all means to this end. Mambler offers to be bought, but it is to no avail because he still cannot be controlled. As a result, he is a despised and distrusted obstacle. Mambler got where is because of his brilliant practical understand and command of technology, but his criminal dealings and lack of morals made him a wanted fugitive in the

Atlantic Alliance. Queen LaFuentes tolerates his bad behavior because she needs the technology he can provide, but if she then gets the supercomputers and robots she needs, Mambler is toast. His devious mind must plan accordingly, but the others are aware of his moves. It appears that Mambler is trapped. His only hope is for some final, useful deal.

Vlatka Maylin is Liu Hyun's head of foreign intelligence operations. She is appropriately devious, cunning, unscrupulous, manipulative, and uses people, who are always treated as objects and the means to her ends. In short, she is perfect for the job. She is ambitious, trusts nobody, expects to be double-crossed, and acts accordingly. She is intent on defeating anyone and everyone she deals with, and to indiscriminately sabotage, negate, discredit, and oppose them no matter what their purpose is and regardless of whether or not they are an obstacle, all for her own self-protection.

Theodore Mitchell is Liu's Attack Dog. He is a manipulative bully with a threatening stare, a harsh tone, and vicious, hurtful words. He may gain what his boss wants in the short run, but at the cost of alienating his victims, who become filled with bitterness and resentment and plot to get even someday. If it becomes necessary to mend any of these fences it will prove difficult, and he will be extremely resistant to making the move. This makes Mitchell an expendable sacrificial lamb to Liu if and when he is no longer useful, and he knows it. He desperately needs some compromising evidence about the boss, something that will gain him some measure of security. Although he craves becoming the top dog himself, his strategy for the time being is to effectively operate behind the scenes, and then aggressively spring into action and seize the opportunity if and when it arises. Of course, Liu instinctively understands this dynamic and keeps Mitchell on a short leash.

Van Newman: As magnificus' computer and artificial intelligence expert, Newman has to be a logical, linear, pragmatic thinker. He has to adopt more flexible standards than other magnificus (other than Annie) are willing to in order to overcome the obstacles to the mission that Earth presents. The natural outcome is that the intuitive portion of his mind is somewhat suppressed. Naturally, the unconscious compensates for this imbalance, and as a result Newman is something of a mischievous schemer. He is pragmatic, and is willing, he hopes temporarily, to stoop to a lower level in order for all of them to succeed on their mission. This sometimes brings him into conflict Carson and the others. Newman is focused and dedicated to his work. It satisfies his talents and his ego, and on the whole, he is satisfied with his role and his station in life.

Benjamin Richards: Megan gives him the personal touch and responsiveness he needs, but she demands his obsessive commitment to her, which is difficult for him, but he needs her as well and so he does his best. She is a worthy partner, but her insatiable appetite for attention can sometimes be oppressive and distracts him from his various projects. Richards is a straight-forward, rebellious, independent and aloof, self-motivated, intelligent, creative, and introverted non-conformist, who occasionally gets wrapped up in his own philosophizing (actually, self-justification). His integrity is absolute. He tends to discount and be oblivious to outside threats. He can sometimes get totally wrapped up in personal projects to the exclusion of all else, until he begins to miss the human touch. Then, after a fix, he will go back to what he was doing before. He is private, but will freely share when prompted. He strives, quite unsuccessfully, not to need anyone else.

Rosa: Rosa is Queen LaFuentes' overly ambitious sister, who wants desperately to off the queen and take the throne herself. She has some brains, but is not a natural plotter and schemer, so she needs help and will accept any credible deal offered to her. In fact, she makes herself available to any internal foe of the queen or outside bloc she can strike a deal with.

Jack Ross: As spokesman and lobbyist for the Game and Robot Manufacturer's Association and prior to that, a gaming and computer genius, he attained his current position because he is brilliant at designing and implementing games, as well as a grand master gamer. He originated most of the Alliance's officially sanctioned games himself. He is cunning and obsessed with outsmarting, manipulating, out-maneuvering, defeating, and triumphing over others, not only in a game setting but in everything. He is a master strategist. All of life is a game to him. His current role of selling new games and finding ways for the manufacturers to cash in is just one more game. Professional and personal relationships both are merely battles of one-upmanship and a fight for dominance. With every fresh victory his ego inflates that much more. He tries to disguise his permanent smirk, knowing that he is better than all the rest, but it is difficult to hide. The more he wins, the more obsessive and inflated he becomes. His currencies are wins, points, prizes, and undefeatable influence. There is no concept of ethics, morality, or integrity except as it pertains to literally and strictly following the game rules; Gaming is the only world that exists for him. His ethics are to win by any allowable means according to the rules. He is compelled to keep playing, because there is always a challenger, and no success is ever the final triumph that delivers him to nirvana. There is a bottomless empty pit at his core, but as long as he is shoveling bucket loads of game winnings into it he doesn't notice. It's a treadmill that will never stop. Could magnificus be his next lucrative market? Could they spread the gaming gospel and Ross' influence throughout the universe? Is there a possible alliance there?

Robert Taylor, Jr. The Atlantic Alliance Economics Minister, has his eye on the presidency and more. He presents himself as an honest politician, one the people should want and support. But he is anything but. Fortunately for him, he is good at hiding his dealings and at finding ways to blackmail or silence anyone who might want to expose him. Since his base is the Economics Ministry, and since money is power, he uses his position to gain control, influence, graft, and payola, attaining more and more skill and experience as he goes. Certainly, Wright senses he is a threat. He follows the creed of the ruthless politician: trust nobody, always have some dirt on dangerous enemies such as compromising them or arranging and documenting bribes or other scandals they can be blackmailed for, discredit rivals, always cover your backside, maintain credible deniability, always have a scapegoat at the ready, stay in the spotlight and crank out favorable propaganda at every opportunity, and finally, tell people what they want to hear, pose as the savior, but then do what you intended to in the first place and spin it as if you are watching out for your target audience.

Joseph Witherspoon is an adventurer and explorer at heart. Overcoming dangerous and challenging situations motivates him. He derives pleasure from the only such avenues available to him: gaming and a hazardous job. Joseph is intrigued by the unconventional and doesn't hesitate to put himself into situations with possible adverse or unexpected consequences such as real face-to-face encounters.

Megan Witherspoon: Separating children from their parents at birth and teaching them to be dependent on state babysitters and social and gaming media, and on instant messaging with their handlers and peers for their relationships, results in a certain degree of neediness and insecurity, and Megan is no exception. Offering politicians as role models in exchange for parents doesn't help, either. As a result of this, she isn't entirely satisfied with her life and craves more overt love, attention, reassurance, and appreciation. If this is not forthcoming, she feels deflated and depressed. Because of this dissatisfaction, she is attracted to rebel types. Megan has transferred her hopes and dreams onto Benjamin Richards, whom she clings to, takes her cues from, and willingly follows. Since true, authentic, personal, love was what she craved, Richards' plain unhidden nature opened a window. Thus, a dependency developed, but at least it was so much better than what she had before. Quiet and reserved around strangers, Megan is sensitive to her own and others' feelings, and seeks and cares about close friends. Professionally, she is meticulous and hard working on projects that reinforce her ego and sense of self-worth, but may give minimal attention to tasks that don't have such a payoff.

Martin Wright, The Atlantic Alliance acting president, has undergone a personal journey. At first, he unquestioningly followed in his father's footsteps, establishing a successful political career that him rise to Chairman of the Atlantic Alliance Legislature. However, both he and his father had eyes for the Presidential Palace. Wright got his start as a loyal staffer to former President Swift, which catapulted him to a legislative position. When Swift died suddenly under mysterious circumstances, it was up to the legislature to elect a successor, but at the same time the constitution specified the Chairman of the Legislature was acting president in the meantime. All Wright needed to do was block every other nomination for the job with help from his allies to become president for life, at the same time preparing unwelcome consequences for those who dared to challenge him.

Wright was definitely not a sparkling, dazzling, or inspirational leader, but rather an accomplished political hack. Nevertheless, he did have some limited and unremarkable capacity for detailed, deliberative decision making. He was never someone who galvanized the emotions of crowds and naturally inspired followers even during a crisis, but he did gather enough followers due to his political and self-promotional skills. PR, spin, backroom deals, and other tools of the trade helped maintain and consolidate his power. He was driven by a thirst for absolute power and control, and he was willing to climb over anyone and go to any lengths to get it. His ego chafes under any restrictions the legislature might dare to try to place on him.

Addendum Two
Elements of the Story

<u>Persona</u>:
Persona has been defined as "the social face of the ego" and as "the face or mask the individual presents to others". It is similar to the "false self." Every profession has its own persona and so does every kind of relationship (for example, mentor, marriage partner, parent, or child). Thus, most people have several different personas.

Persona is necessary for the primitive, archaic, mostly unconscious, impulsive psyche to organize itself and interact constructively with the outside world. It can be a healthy adaptation. But it is also a tool instinctively used by the ego to protect, promote, and glorify itself, and this process is often carried too far, becoming decidedly unhealthy.

Avatars as they appear in the story embody a consciously constructed version of persona with unconscious elements.

According to the psychological literature, the ego and its persona defends itself through the well-known phenomena of projection, rationalization, dissociation, adherence to psychologically useful but false beliefs, and the formation of phobias, obsessions, and compulsions. Disowned defects of the individual are projected onto bogeymen who are villainized without mercy. False external scapegoats are found and harshly treated in an obsessive, single-minded manner.

Conflict between personae and what is termed the "Self" or "true self" can lead people to feel that they don't "measure up" and result in self-inflicted punishment, that is, in self-destructive behaviors and self-flagellation. If on the other hand the personae are stronger than the true self, however that is defined, the ego will project these discrepancies onto others and punish them for their perceived transgressions.

An entire nation or group or faction can enter this latter delusional state. The internal conflict between the personae and the Self can become externalized as a social or political phenomenon and be the source of a mass neurosis. A mild version of this is depicted in the story for both the magnificus and human world,

The ego filters both internal and external events, feelings, and interactions with others, selecting mainly those that reinforce the personae and beliefs it is emotionally invested in. It takes a lot of internal strength to objectively entertain alternative points of view and events that conflict with internal biases. If this process goes too far, the suppression and neglect of internal stimuli, thoughts, and feelings results in one's thoughts and feelings becoming wooden and dogmatic. The entire person then becomes stiff, conformist, shallow, rigid, ritualized, narrow-minded, and unable to emotionally connect to the self or others, in fact, others may become objects, and any sociopathic tendencies are reinforced. Self-awareness may disappear and be replaced by an emotionally determined and ego-controlled false image of the self.

Examples of such a state include stereotyped social groupings, perceived social classes, and game worlds. Some game worlds in the story include such stereotypes. Characteristics of these states include a narrow focus, inviolable rules, artificial constraints, and rigidly defined and enforced socially acceptable, politically correct, iron-clad world views. Virtual worlds and virtual realities thus become paralyzing and self-reinforcing, though comforting, havens for those personae that fit them.

Compliance to such a restricted world limits the potential range of creativity and spontaneity, encourages false relationships, and in the extreme leads to self-loathing or suppression of feelings when a person doesn't measure up to the characters of the game world.

<u>Purpose</u>:

Magnificus taught themselves to value creation itself. Underneath that belief, taken for granted and floating just below the surface of awareness, is a self-serving, unswerving belief in their own superiority and the resulting inescapable conclusion that it is their moral duty to spread themselves and their carefully preserved culture throughout the universe. This represents a cultural blind spot in the story.

By the time of this story, humans have been conditioned to believe that emotional cravings must be uncritically satisfied regardless of their origin, and pleasant neurochemical pathways must be maximally stimulated by any means, and neural pathways leading to depression, anxiety, and other negative emotions must be categorically suppressed. In fact, they have been manipulated into this world view by those who would profit from it.

What is valued naturally flows from instinct and purpose, as interpreted by social norms and customs, upbringing, individual experience. These interpretations tend to be taken for granted and become unexamined and below conscious awareness. Thus, it is that the game world environment and its promotion of values and lifestyle that benefit a ruling elite becomes an environment accepted by most humans with little questioning. The predicament is, do people serve the cultural values, and if so, do they select those values that contribute to the well-being of their fellow humans to the extent they can consciously see and question those culturally determined values, or on the contrary, do they become self-focused, self-serving narcissists, valuing only their own emotional cravings to the detriment of everyone else? These are the extreme cases. Magnificus and humans are meant to represent opposite poles of this range of possibilities.

Maybe there is something of a higher order than the universe, something even grander and more difficult to grasp and which is possibly beyond comprehension or questioning. If that is the case, would seeking it then necessarily be the ultimate purpose of life?

Leadership:

A country or empire can lead by military and economic might for a time, but lasting pre-eminence requires moral leadership. Hubris and belief in entitlement privileges, especially when it results in a lack of effort and airs of superiority, are formulas for disaster. If moral leadership is a "do as I say, not as I do" as practiced by some countries, it is not moral leadership at all. If moral leadership consists of an implicit belief in one's own superiority, as is the case for magnificus, such does not constitute moral leadership either.

Page 172

<u>Group Dynamics</u>:

It has often been observed that the larger the group, the lower its level of confidence and the more it tends towards its lowest common denominator. Groups are often led by their most pathological member, just as families are often forced to cater and respond to their most damaged member.

Some sociologists have observed that, even if a group starts out as an idealistic community service organization focused on an altruistic mission, and is initially led by dedicated founders, it is likely to evolve to become soulless and impersonal over time, and will tend towards serving mainly its own elite. Thus, after a while, the organization debilitates the soul. Size corrupts, and once something is institutionalized it becomes transformed and debased, and the soul cannot be sustained in the face of it.

Is there a way to prevent this evolution? How can freedom of action and pragmatic flexibility be maintained? The stifling effect of rigid, impersonal rules only serves to further extinguish the humanity and spirit from an organization. Harsh environments, persecution, and adversity may preserve some of the original spirit but at the cost of rigidity.

Magnificus faces this problem if their mission of galactic conquest is to remain alive for tens or hundreds of thousands of years and not be turned into a competition among internal groups and special interests.

<u>The Perfection of Virtual Worlds</u>:

Like nuclear power, explosives, drones, drugs, and just about any other technological tool, games and game technology can be a boon or an evil, depending on the motivation of its users and developers. Games can sharpen the intellect and the senses, facilitate education, spark creativity, remotely control useful robots such as firefighting and bomb disabling robots, help close gaps between generations, help people manage their affairs, and have other benefits less easily attainable by other means. Gaming interfaces can be a useful addition to transportation and other machinery. Games and virtual simulations facilitate creativity in ways that were previously unattainable, especially when combined with computational firepower. However, as always, there is a dark side to technology. The unusual thing about games is that many of the abuses are subtle and most of the deleterious effects are in the future, whereas the enjoyment is in the immediate present.

As anyone can observe, some people become addicted to games. Unlike real life, the rewards of gaming are dependable and nearly immediate. Intolerance, the diminishing satisfaction with playing one game can be "safely" dealt with by shifting to another game or a different kind of game.

If computers and robots can handle the practicalities of the real world and satisfy everyone's basic needs, why not pursue the satisfaction of social media and games most of the time? What is wrong with living in virtual fantasy worlds if there is no need to deal with a sometimes unpleasant and unforgiving real world, where intense satisfaction is an infrequent event? Why settle for the delayed satisfaction of long-term efforts and tiring work when immediate gratification is readily at hand? Wouldn't it be a better life to enjoy a fool's virtual paradise than suffer the disappointments of a cruel world when there are no untoward consequences for doing so? In this story we pose the question but leave the reader to answer the question. Perhaps the question is an individual one, and there is no universal answer.

From the point of view of power seeking, controlling elite personalities, games offer a seductive form of manipulation. They can seem to give people what they want and make them happily indebted to the elite, while controlling them and assisting the elite to get some of what it is *they* want. Addicting games and social media plus robots and computers that supply daily needs are bread and circuses on steroids. It seems as if everybody wins, as long as internal psychological reality is held at bay and everyone learns to ignore the inconvenient distinction between reality and fantasy.

But what if an unexpected natural disaster or intentional war, terrorism, malicious action, or outside intervention disables the robots, disrupts the fantasy and destroys the environment, or disrupts the food supply, as happens in this story? What happens to the future of civilization when humans evolve social and gamer capabilities and affinities while losing the interest and capacity for practical survival? What happens when the resources to build and maintain the machines become scarce?

Game culture means that there is no moral development, only the rules and goals pertaining to each individual game; goals and constraints to thinking based on game rules and obstacles are artificial but must be unquestionably accepted by the gamer; thinking is strictly in terms of game concepts with an accompanying lack of flexibility; creativity is encouraged only within the game space; since games are short term goal oriented and strategies are short term, there is no withholding of satisfaction for a greater purpose and no truly long term view; there is no self-discovery and only outer, not inner spaces are explored; there is no provision for recognizing or handling inner psychic conflicts and thus games are a breeding ground for neurosis; broader archetypal concepts and motives may be suppressed or stifled in favor of gaming rewards leading to a lack of psychic balance; games do not lead to moderation because they promote one-track pursuits; the emphasis is on what the gamer wants versus what the world needs; the emphasis on immediate gratification, feedback, and reinforcement diminishes the ability of the gamer to cope with difficult or multi-faceted causes with accompanying major setbacks; the social interactions are a result of game goals and occur in a game context so that narcissism prevails; learning games spoon-feed knowledge and skills with reward pellets in a way that does not lead to valuing knowledge for its own sake; and finally, gaming worlds lack broad and nuanced perspectives and blur the distinction between reality and fantasy. Where is the counter-balancing broad perspective and long-term view?

<u>Cooperation versus Competition and Individual Cheating</u>:

In this story, which species tends more towards cooperation and which tends more toward selfish behavior? Or is there a mixture of both in each case? Under what circumstances is one kind of behavior triggered versus the other? Evolution and environment, natural or artificial, will determine the tendencies.

There can sometimes be a runaway evolutionary process where either cooperation or, more often, selfishness, comes to predominate group behavior. Here, magnificus comes from a cold, harsh planetary environment where cooperation was at a premium. Humans not so much.

Outcomes vary in complex ways depending on the scarcity, abundance, and dependability of the reward, and whether attainment of the reward demands cooperative action. The end result of behavioral evolution also depends on whether the rewards and rules of the game change over time. Fishing by national groups, depletion of the oceans, changing and competitive national commercial fishing laws, and so on is but one example.

When the participants can intentionally alter the rules, probabilities, and relative payoffs, the situation can become quite complicated.

Add to that the ability for deception and intrigue which rewards selfish behavior, or on the other hand, the value of shifting social alliances, plus the fact that relative rewards could vary with time, circumstances, and extraneous factors, and it is a very fluid and non-deterministic evolutionary path.

As an example, see Stewart and Plotkin in the Proceedings of the National Academy of Sciences.

By nature, magnificus is skilled in creating, organizing and adapting group effort. Individuals find great personal satisfaction in identifying with groups and their goals. It is his first instinct. Homo, however, rather than naturally subordinating himself to the groups he belongs to, wants to dominate and control them, and to destroy them if they oppose his personal ambitions. This creates another unconscious disconnect and impediment in the relationship between the two species.

<u>Spin</u>:

Spin works. Propaganda and control of the media works. That is, it works when it is designed to tap into popular emotional biases and prejudices, or when it is associated with unconscious wishes and needs such as ego flattery.

Reality:

To a great extent, the political class has the power to shape reality to its liking. Within limits, it can control people and events to its taste, extracting the material and psychic needs it desires, crushing anyone and anything that stands in its way. This class of people doesn't have to struggle that much. But neurotic obsession, compulsion, etc. can never be satisfied, always wanting still more, and forever escalating until it breaks the barrier of practical possibility; then it suddenly crashes and shatters.

Ethics:

Carson feels it is strategic to wait to inform Earth of the factory ships and the anticipated arrival of another mother ship. He feels that disclosing this information too soon will complicate negotiations to the point that reaching an agreement will become too problematic and therefore impossible. While Carson is truthful concerning magnificus' intentions, is this withholding of important information dishonest, or is it justifiable and understandable? Is it wise or is it counterproductive? Is it ethical? When Earth is inevitably informed of these undisclosed facts, what will their reaction be? Will they feel they have been duped, there are more such disclosures to come, and will they suspect magnificus has sinister ulterior motives? Will all trust be destroyed?

Artificial Intelligence Run Amok:

Per Carl Jung, objective and subjective are inseparable sides of the same coin (the subjective without the objective is insanity; the objective without the subjective is meaningless). Behavior springs from instincts expressed as archetypes, these archetypes are the well springs of motivation and behavior, and the criteria that guide behavior are derived from the set of archetypes as they interact with always changing environment, culture, and personal experience. This is said to be universal, and thus, intelligence must always make a choice. Choices always boil down to subjective preferences, goals that motivate action.

Biologically, "form follows function" as explained by Mambler in the story. Instincts, archetypes, and objectives, or whatever you call them, arise in adaptation to a particular niche in a particular environment and a particular set of circumstances. Consequently, they are situational and ad hoc. Some will inevitably conflict with each other when circumstances trigger them.

For an artificial intelligence, the goals and behavioral criteria derived from them are ultimately provided by a user and are based on the user's objectives. That is, for the machine to do something rather than just sit there, it has to be given a task and this task must derive from subjective motives. It is practical and convenient (but not absolutely necessary) if machine goals are expressed objectively, for example, defined as minimizing or maximizing some state variable(s), as discovering the value(s) of an attribute, as performing some action to a specified standard, as setting an attribute of some entity(s) to a specific value, and so on. But again, the ultimate source of the machine's actions is the subjective desires of a human user.

Based on these considerations, we view intelligence as a practical tool evolved to enhance survival. Ultimate intelligence can then be defined as the ability to satisfy an arbitrary set of time-constrained goals in the presence of varying environmental, resource, and other constraints with maximum effectiveness, maximum flexibility, and minimum risk, in a way that can conceive of and select from the widest range of potential responses, and in a way that results in enhancement or at least minimum impairment of future goal satisfaction, and which can allow for a displacement and time interval between goals and their satisfaction.

An artificial intelligence engine therefore bases its actions on formulated goals, problems the computer is tasked with solving, that is the machine equivalent of Jung's archetypes or Freud's instincts. Any generalized artificial intelligence engine design must follow directly from this definition.

There will always be resource limitations. Suppose you want to write a computer program to play chess. Your first inclination might be to write a program which would systematically examine all possible moves. For each of these possible moves, it would construct a list of possible countermoves by the opponent. For each of these countermoves, it would consider each possible response it could make, and so on, until the game was over. All of the possible outcomes would be weighted for desirability, and the most desirable move would then be selected. The problem is, unless there are only a few pieces left on the board, it would take more time than the age of the universe for the computer to examine every possible sequence of moves in advance. So, it is necessary to use some shortcuts (i.e., "heuristics") to reduce the number of moves examined. The computer must somehow pre-select the moves with the highest likelihood of success and examine only those. Of course, it may well turn out that the best possible move was one the computer failed to consider. These heuristics are a practical necessity, but their effect is usually to trade efficiency for perfection, as in this example. Heuristics usually make the practical application of intelligence possible at the expense of reducing that intelligence; thus, the necessary use of heuristics can be a significant and unavoidable source of error.

As but one example, pattern recognition is heavily used and an important heuristic technique for machine learning, model construction, classification, identification of objects or concepts, problem solving and other uses. However, there are many nuances and pitfalls associated with it. (It is beyond the scope of this summary to elaborate here.)

Unlimited intelligence requires infinite time, limitless processing power, and unrestricted memory, and is therefore a practical impossibility.

Note also that the mind works by constructing models from a basic set of primitive percepts. Machines must do the same. If you think you know the Empire State Building you don't. The real thing doesn't exist anywhere in your mind. If it did, it would be rather painful. Philosophers have a field day with this.

Of necessity the mind constructs, manipulates, and uses models to be able to understand the real world and accomplish its objectives. Intelligent computers must do the same. Logic and math are techniques that operate on models. They do not operate on the real world.

Since the foundation of human and machine intelligence is necessarily subjective, and those subjective imperatives are derived from practical necessity, there is no way to guarantee consistency and avoid internal conflicts in all but extremely simple cases.

As with humans, sub-goals, beliefs, methodologies are built up on this foundation as a result of problem-solving experience and observation. Further structure, methodology, and conceptualization is learned hierarchically. Thus, changing the structure of beliefs and methodologies ("schemas") can easily knock the pegs out from under structures built on top of them, and can thus be potentially quite difficult or catastrophic. Changing the subjective motives, rewards, and assumptions at the root of the machine can easily destroy the functioning of the machine (or psyche).

Since the foundation of any intelligence is necessarily subjective and ad hoc, internal self-consistency is extremely unlikely. The foundation doesn't have to be, and in all likelihood isn't, self-consistent, and internal conflicts and contradictions are bound to occur for any kind of intelligence.

There is another consideration, that is, the structure of the basic objectives, which amplifies the above problem. Instincts can be rigid and exact, as with insects, or they can be more amorphous patterns, which allows behavior to be flexible, adaptable, and dynamic, but which leads to potential pitfalls, mistakes, and errors.

Will artificial intelligences run amok because of their inevitable internal conflicts, increasing rigidities, and practical limitations? Absolutely.

This brief summary is clarified and expanded upon in another story.